FORBIDDEN SEDUCTION

FORBIDDEN #6

R.L. KENDERSON

FORBIDDEN SEDUCTION

SEVEN-YEAR-OLD DEMI CROSS sat at her grandmother's feet and listened to her monthly talk.

"Demi, what do you do if you ever come across a shifter?" Grandmother Cross asked from her rocking chair.

Demi hated these questions. It was the same ones over and over. "I get as far away as possible from them."

"Why?"

Demi looked down at her shoes and fiddled with her laces. "Because I'm half-human, and they will know."

"And how will they know?"

Demi wrinkled her nose up. "They will smell me."

"That's right. We can never be too careful. Until you're old enough to work on covering up your scent, you need to stay away from shifters. I don't know what they will do to you if they find out, Demi, but there are ones who speak of keeping the line human-free and pure. We can never let them find out about you."

Because of these talks, Demi used to be afraid of shifters even though that was what her grandma was. Her daddy was a cat-shifter, and her mommy was human. But, when Demi was one, her daddy had died in a car accident. Her mommy had been worried about Demi's shifter half, so they had come to live with Daddy's mom.

Demi never understood how Grandmother was her daddy's mom. She'd seen pictures of her daddy, and he looked young, like her mommy, although Mommy had said he was nine years older. But Grandmother was old. Demi's other grandma, her mommy's mom, didn't look as wrinkly or mean. Demi's mommy had told her that Grandmother was older when she'd had her daddy, but Demi was never supposed to say that to her grandmother. Mommy had said it would be rude.

What Demi didn't say was that there was a new kid at her school who was a wolf-shifter. Demi had tried to stay far away from him, like Grandmother had said, but he was in her class, and her teacher had made them reading partners. She'd been so afraid the boy would point his finger at her and tell the whole class what she was, but he didn't. All he'd ever said was that she smelled different.

She always wondered what she smelled like. Demi had gotten an excellent sense of smell from her daddy. She knew what humans smelled like and what shifters smelled like. But she couldn't smell herself. And she had never met another half-human/half-shifter. She'd asked her grandmother what she smelled like once, but all her grandmother had said was that she smelled like a halfling.

But the boy at school had said she smelled different. She wanted to ask him more questions, but she knew her grandmother would be mad if she let the boy know that she knew he was a shifter, so Demi kept her mouth closed.

"What if a new kid joins my class and he's a shifter?"

Her grandmother stopped rocking and looked down at Demi. She had the frown on her face that Demi didn't like. It made her look mean. "Why? Did a new student join your class, Demi?"

Demi panicked and lied, "No, he joined another class."

Her grandmother started rocking again. "That's good. There is nothing we can do about shifters in your school, but I can make sure they're not in your class." Grandmother sighed and shook her head. "If only your mother would homeschool you."

Yuck. Demi didn't want to be homeschooled. She had friends at her school, including her best friend, Siya. Demi was lucky though because her mommy worked two jobs, so she couldn't stay home with Demi all day.

Her grandmother looked down at her. "Tell me the rules again."

Demi held in her sigh, so her grandmother wouldn't get mad. "Number one: stay away from shifters. Number two…"

ONE

TWENTY-FIVE YEARS LATER

SAXON EINAR LEANED against the wall of Club Seduction, hands in his pockets and one foot crossed over the other. He was watching the clientele move throughout the large space as he looked for the right kind of female when he spotted *her* instead.

She was not the kind of female he was looking for. Not for him and not for this club. While most female patrons wore little clothing—one, because it attracted attention, and two, because it was hot in the club—this particular woman looked like she was coming home from work. Her skirt was too long, her blouse too buttoned up, her blonde hair pulled back too tightly, and her heels too low. And she was too young and too alone.

She stood out among the rest of the crowd and not in a good way. Saxon told himself to let it go. She was a big girl. But then he saw a group of young guys looking and pointing at her.

He sighed. The sentinel in him was too ingrained, and he couldn't leave her vulnerable even if she wasn't a shifter.

He pushed off from the wall and pulled his hands from his pockets. "Excuse me. Miss?" he said from behind her.

She spun around, and Saxon felt his heart skip a beat. He rubbed his chest. Her scent. It was…different. She was definitely human, but she didn't smell like any human he'd met before. She also smelled flowery and feminine.

"Yes?" she asked.

He dropped his hand and squared his shoulders. "You really shouldn't be here."

She laughed.

"Miss, it's not funny. You don't belong in a place like this."

She put her hand on her hip and narrowed her brown eyes. "The name is Demi, not miss, and how do you know where I belong?"

Jesus. Full of attitude, this one.

Why he'd thought she'd be grateful that someone was watching out for her, he didn't know.

"This club is not your usual scene. If you're looking for a glass of wine and a nice guy to chat up, this isn't the place." He debated on whether or not to say the next part, but he figured she needed a reality check. "People come here to fuck. You're not going to find your next boyfriend here."

☾

Demi pulled the clip out of her updo and let her hair fall down across her shoulder.

Ah…

6

That felt so good after a long day at work.

She looked at the tall, large man in front of her. He had unusual brown-and-blond-striped hair, intense green eyes, and a soul patch under his thick bottom lip. She hadn't known guys even sported those anymore, but it worked on him.

She took a deep breath. *Shifter*. Cat-shifter to be exact. He smelled like the woods her grandmother would take her to when she was a girl.

Her hormones surged, and the male's nostrils flared.

She was already crawling out of her skin with the need to have sex, and her cat liked the strong, virile man in front of her.

But she knew what he saw. She wasn't dressed right, and everyone always thought she was a lot younger than her thirty-two years.

"Listen, you have no idea what I want." *Or what I need*.

And she *needed* to get laid. Due to her human DNA, she ovulated and got her period every month, like any other human woman would. But, because of her shifter DNA, she also went into heat. It wasn't as bad as a heat that a full shifter female went through, but Demi's body still demanded she have sex, or her cravings would become painful.

There were ways around it. She could medicate herself, but she really only needed to get laid once a month, and she was fine. Her heat didn't last for days, like a shifter, which was a blessing. And, thanks to birth control, she didn't actually ovulate, and her heat was a little less intense. It would be nice if it went away altogether, but that wasn't going to happen until menopause.

She'd just settled into a good routine with her last friend

with benefits. *Friend* was a generous term. They were more like acquaintances with benefits. He'd finally stopped asking to go to her place because she didn't let anyone come over. He'd let her drop by whenever she called. She hated to use the term for a human, but she'd had him trained. Then, he'd had to go and meet someone, and now, their once-a-month hook-up was off the table.

That was what had brought Demi to the club to look for a replacement. And she didn't need this guy getting in her way.

He stepped closer. "You don't understand. You could get hurt here."

She put her hand on his strong chest, and he clenched his jaw.

"Look…what's your name?"

"Saxon."

"Look, Saxon, I appreciate your concern. But I'll be fine. I'm a lot stronger than I look." She took a step back. "Now, if you'll excuse—"

☾

The only reason Saxon pulled her into his arms and kissed her was because she couldn't seem to get it through her thick skull that this wasn't the place for her and someone might take advantage of her. If he had to be that someone, then so be it.

But he sure hadn't expected her to taste so damn good. Or for her mouth to open under his and for her to suck on his tongue. His cock went hard, and it took all his willpower not to rub it against her.

Goddamn it. He wanted to fuck her now. This was not how this was supposed to go down.

He let himself have one last taste before he put his hands on her biceps and gently set her away from him.

"Next time, the guy is going to want more than a kiss. I suggest you find somewhere more suited to your needs."

Then, he spun and walked away. He had planned to spend the night relaxing before taking someone home at closing, but now, he needed to find a female. He adjusted his aching erection. The sooner, the better.

☽

Good riddance.

Saxon was a jerk who thought he knew what was better for her than she did. He didn't even know her, and he'd assumed what kind of person she was.

Demi knew she looked out of place, but she hadn't had time to go home and change. Her need was getting stronger, and contrary to what Saxon thought, she wasn't looking for a boyfriend. Who cared how she looked?

She set off in the opposite direction to find someone to take her home. There were couples, threesomes, and groups even larger than that making out around the room, but it didn't faze her.

Demi knew she looked like a librarian because she actually was one, but that was her job and only one part of who she was. She'd been to Club Seduction before, and there wasn't anything she hadn't seen.

She went over to the bar to get a drink. Maybe that would cool her head. Saxon's kiss still lingered on her lips, and she could feel where his soul patch had scratched her chin.

Damn. It wasn't fair that he was such a good kisser.

Her traitorous mind began to wonder what else he could do with his body if he could kiss like that.

A guy sitting on a barstool at the counter smiled at her, and she smiled back.

"Hey," he said.

"Hey."

"You need a drink?"

"I do."

"What can I order for you?"

She paused and then shouted to the bartender, "A rum and Coke, please." She looked back at the guy and held out her hand. "I'm Demi." *And I can order my own drink.* She didn't want this guy to think she owed him something.

"I'm Brad," he said and shook her hand.

The bartender brought her drink over, and she set her money on the counter before Brad could pay.

Demi studied him to see what he'd do. If he got mad, she was out of there. But Brad smiled and nodded his head as if he was saying, *Good for you*.

The stool on the other side of him opened up. "Would you like to sit?"

"Sure."

☾

Demi took a drink as she tuned Brad out. Not on purpose, but, man, he was boring. And, every time there was movement off to the side, she would look to see if it was the Saxon guy.

It was time to bail on Brad. Her cat wanted nothing to do with him, and truthfully, neither did her human half. He might be in a club that was notorious for one-night stands, but that didn't mean he was good at it.

She picked up her glass and swallowed the rest of her drink. She set it down and hopped off the stool. "Sorry, Brad. I gotta go."

"But—wait—I mean—"

She patted him on the shoulder. "Good luck tonight," she said and walked away.

She made her way to the back of the club, toward the dance floor, keeping her eyes out for someone to rock her world.

Her eyes landed on Saxon talking intimately with a female, and her cat practically purred.

Demi rolled her eyes and thought, *What the hell?* It wasn't like she was going to marry the guy. She'd come here to get laid, and she was positive that Saxon could help her out with that.

She approached the couple, and Saxon straightened.

He raised an eyebrow. "Can I help you with something?" He nodded at the female he'd been speaking to as if to say, *Can't you see I'm busy?*

"I'm sorry," Demi told the woman with much sincerity. She was pretty. She'd find someone else. "But I need Saxon."

The woman looked to Saxon and back to Demi and shrugged. "Okay. We'd just started talking anyway."

The female left, and Saxon scowled at Demi. "What the hell do you want?"

"I need you to fuck me."

TWO

AS SAXON PUSHED Demi into his studio apartment that he kept just outside of Minneapolis for his nights off, he concluded that he was crazy.

He had meant to tell Demi to go find someone else when she asked him to fuck her, but her scent had been wild and…open. It was the only way he could describe it.

He was going to regret this in the morning. This female screamed long-term relationship, and he'd have to let her know that this was a one-time thing, but right now, he didn't care so much.

His cat was one hundred percent on board with fucking this female, and Saxon knew better than to fight his beast. The reason he was a damn good sentinel was because of his instincts—his *animal* instincts—and if he got out of sync with his cat, he couldn't do the things he needed to do to be efficient.

But he wasn't going to coddle Demi either. She wanted him to fuck her. That was exactly what he was going to do.

He pulled his shirt over his head, and she began unbuttoning her blouse. He pulled her into his arms and kissed her as she worked on her top, and he maneuvered them back toward the bed. Finding the zipper on her skirt, he yanked it down, and the material fell to her feet. She kicked it away without any hesitation.

He'd expected some resistance from her or for her to ask him to slow down, but once finished with her buttons, she pulled her shirt off her shoulders and went straight for his pants.

She didn't coyly reach inside. She just pushed his jeans off his hips and grabbed his cock with her whole fist.

"Jesus," he cried out.

Demi dropped to her knees and took him into her mouth.

Holy fuck.

This woman didn't mess around. Maybe he'd misjudged her.

Her mouth was warm and wet, and she knew just the right amount of suction to give. She licked around the area where his barbs would emerge when he came, and his knees almost gave out.

Saxon grabbed on to her hair with both hands and held her head still as he pushed his dick in and out of her mouth. A lot of females hated when he fucked their faces, but Demi moaned around him, and her scent got stronger. She was fucking hot for it.

He could do this all night, but he wasn't completely self-ish. He pulled her to a standing position and pushed her back against the bed.

She flopped back and laughed. "Fuck me like you fucked my mouth."

"A little antsy, aren't we?"

She kicked off her underwear and rotated her pelvis. "You have no idea. Now, get inside me."

Saxon chuckled as he went to his nightstand and grabbed a condom. As he walked back to the foot of the bed, he opened the wrapper and began to slide it on.

Demi smacked the thing out of his hand, and Saxon was momentarily shocked.

"No condom."

He studied her. She looked very serious about this.

He put a knee on the bed, bent down between her knees, and put his nose at the bottom of her thigh. He inhaled her scent as he skimmed his nose up her leg to her crotch. He pushed a finger inside her, coating it with her wetness, and then licked his digit clean just to be sure. She wasn't fertile and therefore not trying to get pregnant. And, since he hated condoms anyway and couldn't catch any STDs, it was a win for him.

He straightened and leaned over her. "Are you sure?"

"Yes," she hissed. "Now, fuck me already."

Saxon chuckled and thrust his cock into her.

☾

"Oh shit," Demi cried out as Saxon's huge cock filled her up and then some.

She'd been so afraid he'd tell her they were going to have sex with a condom, or they weren't going to have sex at all.

She probably would have cried because she'd have to go back to the club and start all over.

Because it wasn't just sex she needed. She needed his seed. Despite taking the pill to prevent any pregnancy, her stupid shifter DNA set out to do that every damn month since she'd turned seventeen. And it knew the way to get her pregnant was for a man to come inside her, so that was what she needed from Saxon to feel normal again and not like a sex-crazed lunatic.

Demi wrapped her legs around his hips, lifting her pelvis off the bed. In all of her years of having sex, she'd never slept with a shifter. She had a feeling she was going to enjoy every minute of it.

Saxon grabbed her legs and unwrapped them from his waist. He put them in front of him and draped them over his shoulders. He pounded into her while he held her body for his taking. Her bottom was still hovering over the bed, making his cock go inside her pussy at an angle that stroked her G-spot.

She was almost afraid to let herself enjoy the feeling. No human had ever been able to thrust long enough to get her off that way, and if she didn't have an orgasm, she was going to be miserable for some time.

Saxon bent her knees and pushed her legs wide, and then he leaned over and touched his nose to hers.

"Quit holding back. You wanted me to fuck you. Let me fuck you already."

She gasped. *How the hell did he know?*

Saxon grinned and bit her lip, and then he pounded into her again. She grabbed on to his back and dug her nails in as she felt her orgasm getting closer.

"Please don't stop," she practically sobbed in his ear. "I'm going to come. Please don't stop."

She was incredibly wet, and their bodies made noise every time he slammed into her. She felt her orgasm was just around the bend, and she tightened her internal muscles to help it along.

"Fuck me," Saxon said. "You keep that up, and I might not last long."

And that was what sent her over the edge. The power she had to make this strong male come, too.

A sweeping, white-hot tingling started from her head and traveled down to her toes. She hadn't climaxed this hard in forever. Her legs shook, and her back arched. Saxon held on, keeping his dick inside her as her body convulsed. He thrust a few more times and bit down on her shoulder before coming inside her.

It was like the icing on the proverbial cake, and Demi decided that, if she died from sex, it wouldn't be a bad way to go. Despite his cum being warm, it left a cooling sensation in her, and she knew her body would be satisfied for another month.

Saxon rolled over, pulling her on top of him. She knew about the barbs from her grandmother's crash course in biology and suspected that Saxon didn't want to pull out until his subsided. She was extremely curious, but she couldn't let him know that she knew he was a shifter. It would lead to too many questions, so she clenched her muscles around him.

He groaned. "What the hell?"

She laughed. "Sorry. I just wanted to feel you inside me."

Saxon groaned again and threw a forearm over his eyes. "Fuck me."

"What?"

He pulled his arm away and looked down at her. "I was going to kick you out after this, but now, I might need to fuck you again."

She tightened her muscles again and moaned. "Would that be so bad?"

Saxon lifted her chin and kissed her. "Normally, I'd say yes, but tonight, I'm going to go with no."

THREE

ONE MONTH LATER

SAXON LOOKED around Club Seduction for no one in particular.

Ha, his brain mocked him. That was a lie.

He was there for Demi.

One month ago, he'd awoken the next morning to find her gone without a note or anything else to say she'd been there, except for her scent on his sheets and skin.

He'd meant to kick her out after they had sex for the third time, but he'd fallen asleep. Amateur move. If he let females sleep over, they often thought he wanted more than one night. And that always ended up being more trouble than it was worth.

But Demi hadn't been cooking him breakfast in his kitchen or pretending to be asleep when, in reality, she'd gone to the bathroom and brushed her teeth and put on her makeup. She hadn't even left him a note to call her. Not even a note to say she'd had a good time.

He'd woken up with the biggest grin on his face, thinking he'd won the one-night-stand lottery.

Except he hadn't been able to stop thinking about her. To be clear, he couldn't stop thinking about *fucking* her again. He didn't want to mate with the woman or anything.

But he had been coming every Friday for the last four weeks, hoping to see her again. The fact that he hadn't only made him want her more.

He threw back the beer he'd been nursing, and as it was now warm, he tossed the bottle in the nearby garbage. He'd been there long enough, and he was getting tired.

He headed for the door when he bumped into someone as he tried to get around a group of people blocking the walkway.

"Excuse me," he said to the female.

She turned around and smiled when she saw him. "Well, hello there."

Saxon smiled politely. "Hello." He tried to move past her.

The woman put her hands on his chest. "Where are you going so fast?"

He didn't want to deal with this right now. He looked up and away from the lady.

And he spotted Demi, coming through the front door.

He grinned and turned back to the female in front of him. "See that woman over there?" he said, pointing to Demi. "That's where I'm headed so fast."

He squeezed past the woman with his eyes on Demi.

She didn't see him until he was close, and when she looked up, her eyes widened, and she stopped in her tracks.

"I'm out of here. You comin'?" he said as he approached her.

She nodded, and he took her elbow and spun her around.

"Let's go then."

Saxon took her back to his place and straight to his bed. He fucked her twice before falling asleep.

When he woke up in the morning, he was alone again, leaving him wearing nothing but a grin.

☾

ANOTHER MONTH LATER

Demi walked into Club Seduction, hoping that Saxon would take her with him right away again.

It had saved her so much time. They'd already had sex. She didn't have to worry about condoms. And he fucked her good.

But, tonight, he wasn't there. At least, not near the entrance.

She sighed and headed further into the club. She made her away around, not finding Saxon anywhere. Disappointed, she took a deep breath and set out to look for someone else.

She did another round, this time looking for someone to take Saxon's place.

Of course, when she was looking for someone else was when she found him. He was at the bar, talking to another guy. As she strode toward the two men, the bartender set down two shots in front of them.

Demi pushed her way between them, picked up Saxon's shot, and downed it. She turned and faced him, raising an eyebrow.

"Sorry, man, I gotta go," Saxon said to his friend.

"You just got here."

Saxon shrugged. "Sorry." He put his arm around Demi and led her out of the club.

He took her back to his place and screwed her against the door, on his bed, and in the shower. They both fell asleep, but she thankfully woke two hours later.

Using every stealth skill her grandmother had taught her, she quickly but quietly got dressed and left. She went home, fell onto her bed, and slept like someone whose body was completely satisfied.

((

ONE MORE MONTH LATER

Something was going on at Club Seduction tonight because it was busier than usual, which was good for Demi since Saxon wasn't there. She'd checked already. Twice.

She found a group of single guys and picked one to take out onto the dance floor. Her need was catching up to her, but after three months of being satisfied by the same man, she needed to vet any potential one-night stands with a little dancing.

The guy started grinding into her, and his friend followed and started doing the same thing behind her. Demi smiled. She'd never had a threesome, but she was open to trying new things.

Unfortunately, neither of them was the best dancer, and all she could think was that she'd be seriously disappointed in bed, too. Still, she didn't immediately push them away. She gave them a couple of songs because she enjoyed dancing, too.

She was laughing at a dance move the guy in front of her was doing when her need spiked.

What the hell? She'd never experienced something like this before.

Almost as if she'd entered another dimension, Saxon appeared before her. She knew it was just the spotlights, but he looked like he had a halo surrounding him, and her pelvis clenched.

She pushed back the guy who was behind her and jumped into Saxon's arms. She wrapped her legs around his waist and whispered in his ear, "I don't think I can make it to your place."

Saxon carried her off the dance floor to the back of the club and outside. "Fuck, you smell amazing."

Some guy was taking out the garbage, but both of them ignored him. Saxon pushed her up against the wall and took her mouth as he pushed up her skirt, pulled her underwear aside, and pushed two fingers into her.

He growled—a real animal growl—and her cat responded. Being only half-shifter, she didn't often feel her primitive side, but her cat liked the male cat in front of her.

Demi went for his fly, wanting him inside her, as Saxon tore his mouth away.

"Damn, you suddenly smell…" He grinned and shook his head. "Never mind." He pushed her hand away, pulled his cock out, and pushed it inside her.

She sank her nails into his back at his entrance. "Oh, yes. Please, I want it."

Saxon withdrew and thrust inside her again. "More?"

"Yes."

She tightened her grip, and Saxon seemed to be done with taking it slow.

Her body practically molded to the wall behind her as Saxon pounded into her. She held on tight, letting him take her until he exploded inside her. Her body, happy with the gift he had given her, came, too, her eyes drifting shut until it subsided.

"Demi?"

She slowly peeked her eyes open. "Yeah?"

"Can you take your nails out of my back, baby?"

She smiled. "Oh, yeah. Sorry about that." When she pulled her hands away, she saw the tips of her fingers had cat claws, not human fingernails.

She gasped. She had never shifted. Not even a partial shift like this.

"What's wrong?"

She turned her attention to Saxon as she watched her fingers shift back to normal in her peripheral vision. "I made you bleed."

He smirked. "Don't worry about it. I'm a fast healer."

His barbs receded, and he slowly pulled himself from her body. In the dim light over the back door, she watched him tuck his still-hard cock in his pants while she straightened her clothes.

When they both looked presentable again, he put a hand next to her head and looked down at her. "You still coming home with me?"

"Why don't you come home with me this time?"

Saxon raised an eyebrow. "You sure?"

What are you doing, Demi? You cannot invite this shifter back to your home. You're already risking him finding out what you are. I forbid it. Have I taught you nothing?

Demi ignored the voice of her grandmother in her head and answered, "Yes."

☾

The following morning, after Saxon woke to find himself in Demi's bed and not freaking out about it, he got dressed. Demi was still sleeping. He planned to walk out like she always did with him, but something stopped him.

He turned around and sat on the bed. "Demi?" He shook her awake.

"Yeah?" she said with her eyes still closed.

"Where's your phone?"

"Probably in my purse."

Saxon went out to the living room and found the purse on the floor. He opened it, pulled out Demi's phone, and took it back to her.

"Unlock it for me."

That got her eyes to open. "Why?"

"I'm going to give you my number."

She studied him for a few seconds. Then, she unlocked it and handed it over.

He quickly saved his info in her Contacts and gave it back to her. "If you ever run into trouble, you can call me anytime."

Her eyebrows rose. "What kind of trouble am I going to get into?"

He chuckled and shook his head. "I have no idea. All I know is that a voice told me to give you my number. I think it's my protective instincts. And I don't ignore my instincts." Why he was having them for a human, he didn't know, but he didn't fight it.

"You have protective instincts?"

He laughed and stood. "You'd be surprised." He smacked her on the butt because kissing her after giving out his number would give her the wrong idea. "See ya in a month, babe."

FOUR

A COUPLE OF HOURS LATER, Demi was pouring herself another cup of coffee when her front door opened, and her longest and best friend, Siya, breezed through the door, her long, straight black hair trailing behind her.

"Are you ready to go—" Siya stopped when she saw Demi and wrinkled her nose. "Did you just get up?"

"About twenty minutes ago, yes." Demi took a sip of her coffee. "Where are we going again?"

"The farmers market."

"That's right." Her brain was still half-asleep. "Give me forty-five minutes." Demi carried her coffee toward her room.

Siya laughed behind her. "You look like you have sex hair."

Demi stopped and touched the back of her head. It felt like a rat's nest back there. She winced. It was going to be a bitch to comb out.

"Wait a second…" her best friend said suspiciously.

Demi put the most innocent look on her face and turned. "Yes?"

"You have sex hair, and you're in your PJs. Did you let a guy come to your house?" She knew Demi too well.

She rolled her eyes. "Yes. But it's not a big deal."

Siya put her hands on her hips. "The hell it isn't. You don't let anyone stay over." She dropped her hand and gasped. "Is it the same guy you've had sex with the last three months?"

"Yes." Demi turned and headed back to her room.

Siya's steps sounded behind her. "You need to tell me more about this Saxon guy. You've had sex with him four times, and you brought him home. Are you thinking of having sex with him more than once a month?" She knew all about Demi's *sex affliction*.

"No," Demi said as she walked into her room. "He is not the boyfriend type."

Siya jumped on Demi's bed and lay down. "That sucks."

Demi lifted a shoulder. "Nah, I'm good with being single."

It wasn't that she'd never been in a relationship, but it was easier not to be. It always got too hard to hide her heightened senses and her strength, and she was tired of the looks she got about her big appetite. She couldn't let humans know she was part-shifter, and she couldn't let shifters know she was part-human. Good thing she wasn't bitter or anything.

She tilted her head. "Are you sure you want to lie on my bed?"

Siya wrinkled her nose and jumped off. "You haven't washed your sheets yet?"

Demi laughed. "I only had time to make the bed." And she didn't know if she was going to wash them quite yet. She liked the smell of Saxon in her room. There was something very appealing about the cat-shifter.

Speaking of shifter…

"I forgot to tell you."

"What?" Siya said, inspecting her clothes for sex germs or something.

"My hands shifted last night. I mean, it was just the tips of my fingers, but it was crazy."

"Oh my God, your first shift. Was it amazing?"

Demi shrugged. "Not really. It was kind of in the middle of sex, and I had to hide it from Saxon. But that was after I clawed his back. Thankfully, he heals fast."

Siya's dark eyes widened, and she frowned. "Didn't he get blood all over the sheets?"

Demi waved her hand away. "Nah. We were outside the back of the club." She turned, went in her bathroom, and pulled out her hairbrush.

"You had sex outside?"

Demi laughed as she brushed her hair. "You're such a prude, Siya."

Siya crossed her arms over her chest. "I'd love to see how you turned out if you had grown up with conservative Indian parents. They'd be disappointed if they knew I wasn't a virgin. And, if I ever got caught having sex outside, they'd be horrified."

"But you date. They know that."

"Dating is not sex."

"Well, they'd be really disappointed to know that you've *dated* quite a few men," Demi joked.

"Shh…don't tell them."

"Besides, you forget who my grandmother was," Demi said, throwing her brush back in her drawer.

"Your grandma didn't want anyone to know what you are. She never lectured you on sex."

"Okay, this is true. But I feel your pain."

"And that's why we're friends."

Demi laughed. "So true. Now, go wait for me. I'll be out of the shower as fast as I can." She shooed Siya away and closed the bathroom door.

In the shower, she held up her hands and inspected them. They didn't look any different. Not that she'd expected them to.

But she wanted to know if she could shift them again.

Demi focused all her concentration on trying to make claws again, but the reality was, she had no idea what she was doing.

When she had been little, her grandmother had taken her to the woods and tried to teach her to shift. It had never happened. Not even a partial shift. So, last night had been extraordinary in that aspect. If her grandmother were alive, Demi would've called her right away.

Although, knowing her grandmother, she wouldn't have been impressed. She'd have wanted Demi to do more.

Demi refocused her thoughts away from her grandmother and back to her fingers, but no matter what, nothing happened.

She washed her hair as she replayed last night's events. So, she'd been in the middle of sex, so maybe if she recreated that feeling, that would trigger her shift.

Demi thought about Saxon and how sexy he was. Her

hands moved over her breasts and down between her legs. But, before she could get herself too worked up, she envisioned her claws coming out as she stabbed herself in the vagina.

She immediately dropped her arms.

She might heal faster than humans, but getting injured still hurt like a son of a bitch. And she did not want to go to the farmers market with a freshly clawed vagina.

She grimaced.

It was time to call it quits. What was she going to do with a partial shift anyway? Nothing. She led a very normal human life, and she had no need to bring out her animal side.

Demi finished her shower, got dressed, and met Siya in the living room. They went to the farmers market, and then the rest of the weekend went like any other.

By the time Demi went to work on Monday morning, she'd pretty much forgotten about her shift and passed it off as a once-in-a-lifetime incident.

FIVE

THURSDAY NIGHT, Saxon was putting his laundry away when he noticed holes in one of his favorite shirts. He held it up to the light in the window. They were on the back top. There were two sets of five, and they were only about a centimeter thick.

This was the shirt he'd worn the last time he was with Demi. But he had never seen human fingernails make such small holes. Now, he wished he'd examined his back, but he was pretty much healed.

He shrugged. It was probably some weird fluke thing. He rolled his shirt into a ball and threw it in his small trash can he kept in the corner of his room.

Knock, knock.

Saxon turned as Camden stuck his head into their room. "Hey, are you going over to the main house? Sawyer and Kenzie are supposed to get there soon."

Saxon grabbed another article of clothing. "Yeah, as soon as I'm done with this."

He wasn't as thrilled as some of the others to meet

Sawyer and Kenzie's new baby. Call him a jerk, but it was just another kid. First, it was Vaughn, then Phoenix, now Sawyer, and Zane and Isabelle were going to have a baby soon, too. Reid and Tegan were probably next. He didn't understand what everyone got so excited about.

But he respected his fellow sentinels, so he would go over there and meet the new baby because that was what friends did.

Five minutes later, he was on his way. As he entered through the back door, he concluded he was the last to arrive, going by the pile of shoes there.

Tegan came into the kitchen with a glass in her hand. "You look super happy to be here," she said sarcastically as she headed to the fridge and filled up her glass with water.

"Hey, I'm here, aren't I?"

Saxon and Tegan walked into the living room where almost everyone was gathered around Sawyer and Kenzie.

Off to the side of the small crowd, Aidan Llewelyn was playing with a toy truck, but the second he saw Saxon, he threw the toy aside and got to his feet. Aidan ran over to Saxon, and Saxon immediately picked him up.

"Hey, buddy. Do you understand what all the fuss is about?"

Aidan shook his head and put his hands on the outside of Saxon's mouth. He squeezed Saxon's face together and giggled.

"Yeah, you're bored, too, aren't you, buddy?"

Aidan squeezed his face again and laughed harder.

A couple of people turned at the sound of the toddler's laughter.

33

"Hey, Saxon," Vaughn said. "Why don't you give me Aidan? You can go look at the new baby."

"Uh, that's okay—"

Vaughn took his son before Saxon could finish. He knew that Aidan liked him and hoped the kid would throw a fit at being taken away, but he started squeezing his dad's face instead.

Someone pushed Saxon closer to the baby, and he stopped fighting it. The sooner he held her, the sooner he'd be able to hand her over to someone else.

Sawyer turned around with the cheesiest grin on his face, and Saxon almost took a step backward. He'd never seen Sawyer so happy, and Saxon was embarrassed for him.

"Hey, Saxon. We'd like you to meet Zoey."

Saxon carefully took the newborn into his arms and studied her. She wasn't so bad. She had a unique scent to her, and she was pretty cute. Zoey had some peach fuzz on the top of her head, so it was hard to say what color her hair would turn out to be, except that it was light. Her eyes were closed as she slept, not bothered at all that someone else was holding her.

"What do you think, Saxon? You ready for one of those?"

"You shut your mouth, Zane."

Zane laughed.

"Saxon would have to find someone willing to let him father her baby first," Tegan said.

"Ain't that the truth?" Zane agreed.

"I'll have you know, any female would be blessed to have me father her children. But it still doesn't mean it's going to happen," Saxon said.

Zoey wiggled in his arms, and Saxon caught a whiff of her scent again. It reminded him of something or someone.

He lifted the baby toward his nose and inhaled. Yes, there was something…familiar about it. That was odd since this was the first time he'd met Zoey.

He handed her back to Kenzie, so someone else could have a turn, and he hung out a little longer.

He split after about an hour and went back to the bunkhouse where he ran into Ram playing God of War.

Ram still felt like a new addition to the group sometimes, and other times, it felt like he'd been with them for years. He worked well with others but wasn't the friendliest of guys. But neither was Saxon, and ironically, Ram was probably closest to him. Ram didn't like bullshit, just like Saxon didn't, and the vampire was a good fighter and Guardian. Saxon always enjoyed patrolling with him.

"You're not going to go see the baby?" Saxon asked the vampire as he plopped down into the couch.

Ram shook his head, keeping his eyes on the TV. "Nah. It seems weird, ya know. Sawyer, shifter. Kenzie, human. Me, vampire."

"Dante was there along with Naya."

Ram hit a few buttons, and then *YOU ARE DEAD* came across the screen in red letters. "What did you have to say that for? You killed me. And, now, I'd better go over there if Dante's there." With a sigh, Ram threw the controller to Saxon, who caught it. "Next game's yours."

"Have fun," Saxon said.

Ram gave him the finger as he walked out the door.

Saxon enjoyed his time alone for a while but headed to

his room once everyone started coming back from the main house.

Saxon used to share a room with Reid, but then Vaughn and Sawyer had moved out. Phoenix had gone to live with the vampires and her mate, Dante. Zane had gone to live with the wolf-shifters and his mate, Isabelle. Tegan had moved into Reid's room, so that left Ram, Kendall—the wolf-shifter who had taken Zane's place—Camden, and Saxon. Vance had thought Ram needed his own room since he always slept during the day and was up at night. Since Kendall was the only other female besides Tegan, Saxon now shared a room with Camden.

Each bedroom fit two queen-size beds in them, so Saxon never understood why the bunkhouse hadn't been built with twice as many bedrooms. Vance had once said it built camaraderie, or some other BS like that, having them share. But Saxon figured the alpha had done it to save money. Less walls meant less wood and less drywall. But what did Saxon know?

Someday, he would get his own space. If he could just get Camden mated off to someone.

Thankfully, Camden knew he didn't like to be talked to and kept to his side of the room and didn't say much. And, tonight, Camden was working, so Saxon was blessedly alone.

Saxon stripped down to his boxers and slipped into his bed.

As he closed his eyes, baby Zoey floated across his mind, and for some reason, her smell came back to him. It was an odd thing to think about when he was trying to fall asleep, but then another image penetrated his brain.

He pictured Demi's face when he made her come and the way her scent filled the room. And then he thought again about the shirt he'd thrown away earlier in the night.

Saxon sat up in bed.

"*Motherfucker*," he said to his empty room.

She had completely fooled him.

Baby Zoey smelled just like Demi. That was why she didn't smell like any human he'd encountered before, and that was why Zoey smelled familiar.

Demi was half-shifter.

SIX

FRIDAY NIGHTS, the library where Demi worked closed at five in the evening, so she and her assistant often went out for drinks after work. This night was much more relaxing than last Friday when she'd gone to Club Seduction, looking for Saxon. Tonight meant a couple of drinks and greasy appetizers.

Demi had been working with Lena for a few years now, and they tried to go out together on Friday nights once or twice a month.

Tonight, they had decided on the Red Cow. They had the best burgers in all of the Twin Cities area. With only five locations, it was a great place to grab food.

The hostess greeted them at the door. "Two?" she asked, grabbing menus.

"Four," Demi corrected. She always invited Siya to come with, and Lena always invited her best friend, Iris. She turned to Lena. "Unless someone else is coming."

"Nope. Just us four."

Soon after they were seated, the other two ladies showed up.

"I'm starving," Siya said as she sat down next to Demi. "Give me my fries and turkey burger now."

Demi laughed at her friend's fierce look. "Someday, I'm going to try the turkey burger. But today is not that day. I need my beef, and they have too many good choices."

Siya wrinkled up her nose. Raised Indian, she'd grown up a vegetarian. She'd started eating meat when she was in college, but she still didn't eat beef because of her beliefs.

Iris showed up two minutes later, and they ordered their food.

Dinner was delicious, and the company was great.

"I do not know how you clean the rest of our plates every time we go out," Lena said to Demi.

Demi smiled and shrugged. "I have a big appetite."

"Yet you're still a tiny blonde," Iris said.

"She has good genetics," Siya said, and Demi almost choked on her food.

Good genetics? Or something like that.

After they paid their bills, they all headed outside. It was dark now, and the summer temperature had gone down a few degrees.

"Where are you parked?" Demi asked Siya.

"In the alley."

"Me, too."

"I'm parked down the street," Iris said, pointing in one direction.

"Ha. I'm parked the opposite," Lena said.

The Red Cow had excellent food but shitty parking at all locations.

"Well, I guess I'll see you on Monday," Demi said to Lena. Demi worked every fourth Saturday, and it wasn't her weekend to work.

The rest of them all said their good-byes, and Demi and Siya headed down the alley.

"Want to do anything else tonight?" Demi asked.

"Sure. What do you have in mind?"

"I don't know."

"How about you hand over your purses?" a gravelly voice said, coming out from behind the building. A man stepped in front of them, holding a knife.

Siya squeaked and started shaking. Demi could smell the fear coming off her friend.

The man in front of them looked and smelled like he hadn't showered in a long time. His teeth were black. His hair looked like it had once been light but was so full of grease that it was now dark. His eyes were glassy, and he appeared to be strung out.

"Look, sir, I am more than willing to give you some money, but I'm not giving you my purse." It would take her days to cancel and get new copies of everything. Plus, she had some personal items in there that were irreplaceable.

"Demi, I think we should give him what he wants."

"Hell no." Demi took her purse off her shoulder and handed it to Siya. "Hold this."

Siya shook her head, so Demi pushed it against her friend's chest and let go. Siya caught it as Demi stepped forward.

"Look, lady, I don't want to hurt you. Just hand over your bags."

"So, don't hurt me. Leave."

The would-be mugger shook his head. "I need them."

Demi took a step forward. "No, you want them. There's a difference." If she could get close enough, she could take the knife away from the guy.

"Just give them to me," he almost whined.

Demi moved another step closer and shook her head. "I can't do that."

"I need the goddamn purses! Give them to me now!"

The man had suddenly done a complete one-eighty, and Demi knew she wasn't going to reason with him.

She yelled, "Siya, run," as she tackled him.

For being high, the guy fought her hard. Or maybe it was because of the drugs. But Demi knew she was stronger than this human, and she wasn't going to let him steal their stuff. She just hoped Siya had made it to her car.

The guy managed to get on top of Demi and punched her in the face. She saw stars and instinctively responded with the same move. Except she didn't hear a smack as her fist hit him, and she was suddenly covered in a warm liquid, including her eyes.

The man's weight fell on her, and a pain pierced her side.

Damn, he's heavy.

"Oh my God. Demi, are you okay?"

"Siya?"

"Yeah, it's me."

"I told you to run," Demi said as she pushed the guy off of her and wiped her eyes.

"Holy shit."

Demi sat up. "What?" She looked down at herself. She was covered in blood.

41

"Demi, I think you shifted. And I think you killed him."

She looked over to see the drug-addict mugger staring at the sky with a blank look in his eyes, and his neck was torn open from what looked like an animal attack.

Demi scrambled to her feet. "Oh my God." She held up her hand. She had human fingers. "I don't know what happened." She took two steps back and felt light-headed. "I think I'm going to pass out."

Her knees gave out, and Siya tried to catch her.

"Oh my God, Demi. You've been stabbed."

Demi looked to where Siya had lifted up the side of her shirt. "Oh. That's not good," she said with a surprisingly calm voice before she fell on her butt.

"What the hell are we going to do? There's a dead body, and you're covered in blood." Siya pulled her shirt off over her head and pressed it to Demi's wound. "I need to get you to a hospital."

"Do you still have my purse?"

Siya furrowed her brow.

Yeah, she probably sounded crazy, asking for her handbag at a time like this.

"Yes."

"I think…I think you should find my phone and call Saxon."

Her eyebrows went up. "Saxon? As in your booty call Saxon?"

"Yeah."

"Why?"

"Because I think the only person who can get us out of this mess is a shifter." Demi slowly lay on her back on the ground. "I think I'm going to take a nap now."

And that was the last thing she remembered.

☽

Jeff Schultz hit the button on his phone to stop the recording and played it back just to make sure he hadn't imagined things. But there, on his screen, was a fight and what looked like a woman killing a man who'd tried to mug her.

It was dark with minimal lighting in the alley, so Jeff couldn't be sure if the man was dead or not, but there was no mistaking the way the woman had practically ripped the guy's throat out.

His video was TMZ gold.

Jeff turned off his video, sent his friends a text to cancel their plans, and ran back to his car. And, to think, he'd been pissed about having to park so far away. In the end, it was the best thing that had happened to him in a long time. He was going to sell his little video for lots of money, and maybe he'd finally be able to pay back his illegal loan.

SEVEN

SAXON KNOCKED on Ram's door.

"What?" his deep voice grumbled from the other side.

"It's time to get up. We have to go soon."

"Give me five."

Saxon waited in the kitchen, and true to his word, Ram came out five minutes later.

They were working together tonight, and Saxon appreciated Ram's punctuality because he was ready to go.

Saxon had restrained himself from knocking down Demi's door last night and scaring her. But his patience had gotten him nothing because, when he'd gone there this morning, no one had been home.

He'd gone back around noon, but the house had still been empty. He'd reluctantly gone back home to take a nap before he went out on patrol tonight, and now, he was itching to go. It was after nine, and Demi had to come home sometime. He wanted to talk to her about her secret he'd discovered.

"You ready?" Saxon asked the vampire.

"Yep." He grabbed an apple from the fruit bowl and headed for the door.

The two of them climbed into Saxon's SUV and took off.

"Where are we supposed to go first?" Saxon asked Ram.

Ram grabbed his phone and pulled up a list of locations that had been listed as having suspicious activity. There was always a running list of things to look into that the shifters and vampires kept. The list came from members of their species calling into a hotline of sorts that they'd set up and a website they'd recently started. Most things were nothing, but they always had to follow up to make sure neither group was outed to humans.

They were over halfway to their first stop of the night when Saxon's phone rang. He didn't recognize it, but it was a local number.

"Saxon," he said by way of a greeting.

"Oh, thank God. I was afraid you wouldn't answer," a woman said on the other side.

He didn't recognize her voice. "I'm sorry, who is this?"

"My name is Siya. I'm Demi's friend. She's in trouble, and she asked me to call you."

Saxon's instincts went on high alert, as did Ram's. The vampire could probably feel the emotions coming off him.

"Where are you?" Saxon asked and took the next corner a little too fast.

"Red Cow. North Loop location."

"We'll be there in less than ten."

He hung up and threw his phone in the center console. It was a minute later he realized that he hadn't gotten any information and had no idea what he and Ram were walking into.

 ☾

Siya Patel paced back and forth in front of Demi and the guy who'd tried to rob them. She continued to monitor and check on her friend, but she was too wired to sit and wait quietly for Demi's booty call to show up.

Siya really hoped that Demi had told her to make the right call—no pun intended. But, really, there was no other choice. She couldn't call the police. Yes, it had been self-defense, but there was no way to explain what looked like an animal attack in the middle of a large city. They would think Demi had used some kind of weapon.

And Demi needed more medical help than Siya could provide. If only she'd gone to medical school like her parents wanted instead of rebelling by becoming a nurse.

Siya just hoped this Saxon guy could help and that he hurried up. She had managed to pull Demi and the body into the shadows, but someone was bound to walk down the alley at some point.

She had built up a sweat from the physical labor, but since she had used her shirt to tie off Demi's wound, the night air was starting to feel cool against her damp skin. Her hands were also clammy from fear.

Demi's phone rang in her hand, and she nearly dropped it because it'd scared the crap out of her.

It took her three times to swipe it correctly in order to answer.

"Where are you?" the deep voice on the other end said.

She'd only talked to Saxon once, but she already knew this wasn't the same person despite the phone's display saying it was him calling.

"In the alley."

"We're here," the man said and hung up.

A second later, a black SUV came barreling toward her. She sure hoped it was the guy on the phone as she stepped in front of the vehicle, waved her arms, and hoped her boobs didn't fall out of her bra.

They came to a stop about five feet in front of her, and two large men got out. She could only make out their forms with the headlights shining on her eyes.

"Siya?" the driver asked.

"That's me."

"Where is she?" he asked.

Siya knew he meant Demi, so she pointed to the wall behind her. "Over there."

The two came around the front, and she could see them better. Both were tall, as she'd already noted, and muscular. Two someones she—ironically—wouldn't want to meet in a dark alley.

The driver had to be Saxon since Demi had described his two-toned hair to her. He immediately went around Siya and over to Demi.

The other guy was freaking intimidating. He had yellow eyes and a face that said he was all business.

He looked her up and down and pulled his dark T-shirt off. "Put this on," he said as he handed it to her.

"Thank you." She pulled it over her head. It was warm from his body and went almost to her knees. She could wear it as a dress.

"I'm Ram. What happened?" the now-shirtless and very ripped man asked.

"We were leaving the restaurant. This guy came out with a knife and demanded we hand over our purses. I wanted to give them to the guy, but Demi fought him. He stabbed her in the side, but she, um…killed him."

Ram walked past her to the man and tried to find a pulse. "He's dead all right."

Both men straightened, and Saxon pulled out his cell phone. He pushed a couple of buttons and put it to his ear. "Yeah, it's Saxon. We need all hands on deck. The alley next to the Red Cow, North Loop location." Saxon hung up.

"Who are you guys?" Siya asked, mystified.

Saxon tilted his head. "That depends. Do you know what Demi is?"

Siya looked back and forth between the two men, not sure if she should say anything.

"Let's put it this way," Saxon said. "Do you know how this guy died? How he got these marks on his neck?"

Apparently, the cat was out of the bag—again, no pun intended.

"She shifted. Or her hands did anyway. It's only ever happened once before."

"When?"

Siya's eyes widened. She didn't really want to say it out loud, but if he wanted to know, she'd tell him. "Uh…last Friday…when you two were, you know…in back of the club."

Ram looked at Saxon. "Behind the club? You've been holding out."

"Shut up," Saxon responded without much heat. "I need

to get Demi to the infirmary. Can you bring Siya back to the bunkhouse?"

She brought her arms up and waved them back and forth. "Hey, I'm not going anywhere. And Demi needs to go to a hospital."

"No, Demi needs to go to the shifter infirmary. And you can go home after we talk to you. We need to make sure the situation is handled completely. For your friend's sake," Saxon said. "Don't you agree?"

The man had a point, but she didn't know either of them. She looked down at Demi. But her friend had trusted Saxon enough when she knew she was losing consciousness. "Okay."

Saxon picked up Demi without any effort, and Ram opened the back of the SUV, so Saxon could put her in the back.

"She smells like you, man," Ram said. "Did you mark her or something?"

"No," Saxon said and got behind the wheel and took off, leaving Siya alone with Ram.

EIGHT

"WHERE'S YOUR CAR?" Ram Warin asked the little human in front of him.

Her big brown eyes showed every emotion that was in her head, and he liked that he didn't have to guess what she was thinking.

"What about the body?"

The corner of Ram's mouth lifted. "We're not going to leave until backup gets here."

"Oh." She pointed behind her. "Back there. But you should know that Demi drove, too. Should we each take a car? I can follow you."

Ram stepped close and picked up Siya's arm. "You cut yourself." He hadn't noticed with all the other blood that had been spilled that night.

She pulled her arm toward her, so she could see. "Oh. I didn't even know."

Ram picked up her arm again and licked her wound. Her blood was bitter, the opposite of vampire blood, but surprisingly, it didn't taste unappealing. It reminded him of grapefruit. He licked her wound again to make sure he got the whole thing—and to taste her once more. He kind of liked it.

Siya yanked her arm back. "What are you doing?" she asked, her voice full of alarm.

"Healing your wound."

Her brow furrowed. "Shifters can do that?"

"No. I'm a vampire."

Her eyes widened. "You're a vampire?"

Shit.

"Oh. Yeah. I guess I thought you knew."

She shook her head as headlights appeared in the alley. Three SUVs pulled up, and cat-shifter sentinels Tegan, Camden, and Vaughn got out along with Kendall, the wolf-shifter who lived with the cats.

Vance, the cat-shifter alpha, was the last to exit the vehicle, and he immediately assessed the situation. "Camden and Kendall, I want you to take the body up north and work him over. I want the authorities to be confused about whether a wolf or bobcat went after him." He turned to Ram. "You're bringing that young lady back?"

Ram saw Siya frown at the name. "Yes. But we have two cars. I'll drive Siya's."

"Tegan, can you take the other?" Vance asked.

"On it."

"Oh, and call Reid on your way back and ask him to look into security cameras around the area and wipe them if necessary."

"Got it." He looked at Siya. "Keys?"

"Oh, yeah." She went over to the wall of the building and picked up two purses. She rummaged around in one of them and pulled out a set of keys. "Here you go," she said and brought them over to Tegan. "She parked back there," Siya said. "Not sure where."

Tegan smiled. "I'll figure it out. What kind of car?"

Siya told her, and Tegan took off.

"You two, go," Vance said. "Vaughn and I will clean up the mess."

"Thank you," Siya said.

Vance smiled warmly. "You're welcome."

Ram took Siya's hand. "Let's go."

NINE

KENDALL WALKER FOLLOWED Camden into the middle of the trees to dump the body they'd been ordered to bring up there. She was getting bored, and her eyes wandered down to Camden's strong backside.

The blond cat-shifter turned easily despite the weight he carried on one shoulder. "Are you staring at my ass?"

"Yes. I'm bored, and the outdoor scenery is the same thing over and over. Trees, trees, and more trees."

Camden swung back around and continued forward. "Yeah, that's probably a good sign that we can stop." He leaned forward, dropping the dead weight to the ground.

Kendall came up to stand beside him. "I feel bad. This human was someone's son."

Camden shrugged. "Yeah, but it was self-defense. And we can't let anyone find out about us. It's really the only way. Someone will find him eventually."

"It's sad that no one will probably miss him."

Camden looked over at her. "It is, but we didn't choose his life for him, Kendall."

She sighed. "You're right."

"You're not usually this sentimental."

"I know." She lowered her voice. "I think it's hormones. My heat is coming."

"Aw."

She didn't want his male sympathy even if it was coming from a caring place. "Let's do this."

Camden reached for his shirt.

"Wait," she said.

"Why?"

"Let's go a bit away before we take off our clothes. It wouldn't be wise to leave them near the body in case they look for evidence of foul play."

"Smart," Camden said. "Let's go this way."

Kendall followed until Camden stopped. "Far enough?"

"Yeah." She pulled off her top and kicked off her pants.

She looked over at Camden as she took off her underwear and bra. He was already naked, and her eyes strayed to his dick. It was long and thick despite his flaccid state.

But it soon shortened as Camden shifted into his cat form.

I'm definitely near my heat, she thought as she shifted into her wolf.

The two of them headed back for the body. When they reached it, they both stopped and stared at each other.

Kendall barked, telling Camden to go first. The human smelled like body odor, drugs, and now death. She was going to do as little of the damage as possible and hoped Camden would do most of the work.

Camden showed her an impressive set of canines and

shook his big tan head, but he stepped forward and bit down on the body.

Kendall watched for a few minutes before she stepped in to help. She used her claws more than her teeth whenever possible, but it was unavoidable.

She felt like throwing up. She was going to go home, brush her teeth for an hour, and shower for another.

Kendall stepped back from the body. It looked well and mangled, and a few days in the summer heat would also do some damage.

A nudge to her side had her turning to Camden. Once he had her attention, he took off running, and she followed. They continued past their pile of clothes and kept going.

She didn't know how long they ran, but soon, a small body of water appeared before them. Kendall jumped in, mouth open. Once her body was submerged under the water, she shifted back to her human form and sprang up from under the water.

A few seconds later, Camden did the same.

She wrinkled up her nose. "That was disgusting."

"Tell me about it."

"Thanks for bringing me here to rinse off."

"No problem."

"How did you know this was here?" she asked.

Camden walked over to the edge and sat down. "I've been up here a few times when I wanted to be alone."

"Yeah, it gets to be much sometimes, living with so many people."

"Are you doing okay, living with us?"

It might seem like an odd question to ask when they

were both naked, but they were shifters. Nakedness came with the territory.

"Yeah. Everyone's been nice."

Camden laughed. "You'll feel like one of the group soon."

"How do you know I don't already?"

"Because that was way too polite an answer."

Kendall smiled. "You're too smart."

"Nah." Camden lay back and stared at the night sky. "I was just new once."

"I've been living with you all for months."

The corners of Camden's mouth turned up. "But you're still new. Or at least, you feel that way."

"True." Kendall came out of the water, feeling much cleaner, and lay beside him. The stars looked beautiful, and it was very peaceful. "How long do we have before we should get back?"

"I think a few more minutes wouldn't hurt."

Before long, the two of them dozed off. Kendall woke to find herself snuggled against Camden along with his arm around her. She gently rolled away, waking Camden in the process.

He rubbed a hand over his face. "Holy shit. How long did I sleep?"

Kendall sat up. "I have no idea. I fell asleep, too." She ran her hand over her dark locks. "My hair's still damp, so probably not too long."

Camden got up on his hands and knees. "You ready to go find our clothes and get out of here?"

She answered by shifting to her wolf and sprinting away

from Camden. She didn't make it far before she heard pounding footsteps behind her.

They made it to their clothes, shifted back to human, and got dressed. They both checked their phones, but there were no new calls.

As they walked back to the SUV, Kendall said, "Thanks for taking me to the water. It'll save me a lot of time when we get home. Although I still have a hot date planned with my toothbrush."

"You're welcome. Just don't tell anyone else that it's here."

"You don't want them coming up here, or you don't want them teasing you about it?"

"Both, I suppose."

Kendall smiled. "Your secret is safe with me."

"Thanks."

They were almost to their vehicle when Camden said, "Hey, Kendall?"

"Yeah?"

Camden pulled the keys out of his pocket and hit unlock on the key fob. "You need any help with your heat, I'm here."

Kendall smiled. It wasn't a pick-up line, and he wasn't hitting on her. His voice was sincere. And he would be taking a risk, servicing her through her heat, if she accepted. It wasn't just about sex.

"Thanks, Camden," she said as she reached the passenger door.

He nodded and pulled his own open. "I just wanted you to know. You might be new, but you're not alone."

TEN

"WHAT CAN you tell us about your friend?" the older gentleman—who'd introduced himself as Vance, the cat-shifter alpha—asked Siya.

After she'd left the alley with Ram, he had brought her to a building that was apparently a hospital of some sort. It had no markings on the outside and looked like an ordinary building, but she supposed the shifters couldn't announce they had their own hospital.

Inside, the building did look more like a clinic with a reception desk and a waiting room, but that was all she had been able to see before Ram led her to the room she was currently sitting in.

It looked like a small conference room, but it felt more like an interrogation room with the four large men across from her. Vance was sitting directly across from Siya with Saxon to one side and another gentleman—who had to be Vance's son, going by their similar looks—sitting on his other side.

Ram was standing against the wall with his arms crossed.

"So, what is this?" she asked. "Bad cop, good cop, bad cop, good cop?"

Vance smiled. "No cops. You didn't do anything wrong. We just want to know as much about the situation as we can. And that includes your friend."

Siya hesitated.

"We're here to help her."

"Are you sure?"

Vance frowned. "Why would you ask that?"

"Because Demi's grandmother always told her to never let shifters know what she was."

"Why?"

"I don't know exactly. I think her grandmother was afraid you would kill her or something. She said there were shifters who didn't want the bloodline mixed with human blood." Siya shrugged. "But you really need to ask Demi these things. It's all hearsay. Her grandmother never talked about this stuff with me, and Demi always said the lady was a little paranoid."

"That's ridiculous," Vaughn said. "We would never kill someone because they were half-human."

Vance didn't say anything.

Siya sat forward. "You're not really going to kill Demi, are you?" It didn't make sense why they would bring her to a hospital to mend her back to health and then kill her. *Because they can't question a dead person.* Siya's eyes widened. "Does that mean you're going to kill me, too? Since I know about you?" Her eyes darted to Ram for some reason, as if he were the voice of reassurance.

He just tilted his head and studied her.

"We're not going to kill anyone," Vance said.

Siya looked to the leader again and narrowed her eyes. "Then, why didn't you say anything at first?"

"You sure are ballsy for someone who's worried we might kill you," Saxon said.

Siya shrugged. "If you're going to kill me, you're going to kill me. I'd like to go into my murder being as informed as possible."

Ram snorted.

"No one is murdering or killing anyone," Vance said, his voice firm. "But there was a group from a long time ago, who did preach on keeping the bloodlines pure. Untainted of vampire or human, and while the wolves and cats worked together, they wanted their bloodlines separate from each other."

Vaughn laughed. "They must be rolling over in their graves now."

Siya's brow furrowed.

"My mate is a vampire, and we have two children," Vaughn explained when he noticed Siya's confusion. "And then there's Payton and Damien, Phoenix and Dante, Sawyer and Kenzie, and Zane and Isabelle."

"Yes, well, the world is much more progressive now," Vance said. "Do you know how old Demi's grandmother is? Was? And her full name? What are Demi's parents' names?"

"I have no idea about her grandmother," Siya said. "But she looked like she was about two hundred years old the whole time I knew her. She passed away about ten years ago now."

Vaughn snickered.

"I'm sorry. That was probably disrespectful." Siya's mother would be ashamed of her daughter's lack of respect for an elder and the dead. "Her grandmother's name was Lucille, I believe. Lucille Cross. Demi's father died when she was young, but I think his name was Austin. She was mostly raised by her grandmother. Her mother, who was human, was around, but she worked a lot. I think she didn't know what to do with her half-shifter baby. Her name is Sharon Nelson. Demi hasn't seen her for almost a year though. They aren't close."

Vance turned to his son. "Call Reid. Have him dig up anything he can on Lucille Cross, Austin Cross, and Sharon Nelson."

Vaughn pushed back his chair and stood. He pulled his phone from his pocket as he left the room.

"Are you worried that this Lucille knew something we didn't?" Saxon asked.

"I honestly don't know. I don't understand why she would keep her granddaughter's existence from us. Even with the groups that didn't like bloodlines mixed, my father and I have never been against it. I just want to have all the facts."

"Like I said, her grandmother was kind of paranoid. If she had ever found out that I knew about shifters, her head would have probably exploded."

"How do you know?" Saxon asked.

"Demi and I have been friends since kindergarten. She trusted me. But she didn't tell me for years. She knew her grandmother was a little extreme in her thinking, but she also made Demi believe what she was saying. Honestly, I was surprised when she told me to call you tonight," Siya said to Saxon. "She must really trust you."

Saxon looked away when everyone's eyes went to him. He cleared his throat. "Yeah, well, she made the right call."

There was a knock on the door to the room, and it opened. It was Vaughn. "Reid's looking into it. He said he'll call us when he has information, if we're not home by then. And the nurse just came and said Demi's out of surgery."

Siya and Saxon both stood.

"Everything went well, but she's still unconscious. She should be waking up soon."

"Can I see her?" Siya asked. She hadn't realized how worried she was about her friend until that moment. She had taken for granted that her friend was stronger and healed faster.

Vance cleared his throat. "I think it's best if we talk to her first." He looked apologetic. "Why don't you go with Ram and wait in the waiting room? We'll let you know when it's time."

Siya was disappointed, but she understood. Demi had killed someone tonight even if it was in self-defense. "Okay."

"Do you mind if I speak with her first?" Saxon asked.

"No. She might be more open to speaking to you alone," Vance said.

Saxon nodded and left the room. Vance and Vaughn followed, and it was just Siya and Ram again.

"Sorry you're stuck babysitting the human."

Ram shrugged and walked over to her. "It doesn't bother me."

"That doesn't exactly make me feel better."

He raised an eyebrow. "And what would?"

"I don't know. How about, *I'm not babysitting you. I'm keeping you company?*" She tried to mimic his deep voice.

Ram snorted again and took her elbow. "Let's go." He led her to the waiting room and picked a couple of chairs in the corner. "Sit."

She did, suddenly tired.

He glanced around. "Do you need anything?"

Siya shook her head. "Just a bed and pillow. It's past my bedtime."

The corner of Ram's mouth lifted, and he sat. He put his arm around her and guided her head toward his shoulder. "You're going to have to use me for now."

"Are you sure you're okay with that?" she asked sarcastically as she laid her head down.

He responded with mockery of his own. "Sure. You didn't taste that bad."

She held up her arm and inspected her cut. She lifted her head. "Whoa. It's almost healed."

"That's why I licked you. We have healing properties in our saliva."

She looked at him. "Not because you want to drink all my blood?"

He wrinkled his nose. "No way. Vampires feed from vampires." He tilted his head back and forth. "And some feed from shifters. But human blood is weak and doesn't sustain us."

"Gee, thanks." *Nothing like feeling inferior.*

Ram pressed her head back down. "Don't be offended. You outnumber us by the thousands. If you take that into account, your species is stronger."

She rested her head on his shoulder. It felt weird to be so

close to someone she'd just met, yet at the same time, it wasn't strange at all. It must be all the excitement and trauma of the night. She took a deep breath and noticed that Ram smelled almost sweet.

She closed her eyes. "I think I'm just offended that you don't want to drink *my* blood." The evening's festivities must have also made her admit things she wouldn't normally admit.

"Don't worry. I'll still drink your blood when we fuck."

Siya's eyes flew open, and she lifted her head again. "Did you just say what I think you said?"

"Yes," he said in a neutral tone. He didn't even look at her. He was staring at his phone as he swiped through stuff.

"You're pretty cocky."

"No. I speak the truth."

"I don't even know if I want to sleep with you."

"Sure you do. Otherwise, you wouldn't want me to drink your blood." He pushed her head down one more time. "Now, go to sleep. We're not having sex tonight. You can worry about that later."

The guy was crazy, assuming they were going to have sex after only knowing each other a few hours, but to her surprise, she fell asleep anyway.

ELEVEN

DEMI GRUNTED in pain as she woke from unconsciousness. She tried to open her eyes, but it was bright, so she quickly closed them again.

She heard beeping and the air smelled of sanitation. She was in a hospital.

The events of the night came back to her with a swiftness, and she opened her eyes again. She had to know if Siya was okay, and the man who'd tried to mug them…she needed to know what had happened to him.

She looked to the wall and then to the door and realized she wasn't going anywhere.

"How are you feeling?" Saxon asked from the chair next to her bed. His face was grim.

"Like shit." She hadn't even smelled him there.

He leaned forward, putting his elbows on his knees. "That's to be expected, I suppose. You were stabbed in the side. They had to do surgery on you."

Demi looked around again. "What hospital am I in?"

"None. You're at the shifter infirmary." He tilted his head to the side. "Makes sense since you're half-shifter."

"I'm half-human, too, so I could easily be at a human hospital."

"Except we know about humans. Humans don't know about us."

Demi tried to sit up, pushing herself up with her hands, but she was weak.

Saxon stood. "Stop that. You're going to hurt yourself." He pushed a button on the bed, and her head began to rise. "Good?" he asked after a couple of seconds.

She nodded.

He returned to his chair.

"How did you figure out what I was? I'm guessing Siya told you."

"Siya did mention it, but I'd figured it out myself the other night. I always knew you smelled different. I just couldn't put my finger on why."

"What's going to happen to me now?" Demi asked.

At the time, having Siya call Saxon had seemed like the right thing to do. She certainly couldn't call the police with their technology these days. But human jail might not be so bad compared to what the shifters could do to her. She should have insisted Siya run while she stayed to face the consequences because, now, Siya knew about the shifters' existence, too. Her grandmother would have been so disappointed.

"I can handle whatever it is you do to me, but please don't hurt Siya. She's known about me almost her whole life, and she's never spoken a word to anyone."

Saxon scowled. "Your grandmother must have done a real number on you."

She frowned. "What do you mean?"

"We're not savages, Demi. We're not going to hurt you or your friend."

She sighed. *That's a relief.*

"If you thought we'd do something, why'd you call me?"

She shrugged and immediately regretted it. "Ow." *That hurt.* "The lesser of two evils, I guess," she answered his question. "Plus, I'd just been in a fight and gotten stabbed. My rational thinking wasn't exactly up to par."

"I'll say it was. You made the right decision."

"Hmm."

"Did you know I was a sentinel when you had your friend call me? When did you figure it out?"

Her nose wrinkled. "A sentinel?"

He shook his head. "Damn, your grandmother didn't teach you anything, did she?"

"She taught me how to keep my existence a secret. She taught me how to mask my animal scent. I had been doing well the last thirty-two years until I decided to have sex with a shifter. My mistake."

Saxon snorted. "It's the smartest fucking thing you ever did."

"Agree to disagree," she said, looking away.

"Your heat must work differently? Your grandmother must have at least explained that to you."

Demi didn't have a lot of warm feelings for her grand-mother, but she didn't like how Saxon had been speaking about her. "Yes, she did. But she didn't know that I would ovulate and bleed once a month, like a human. My heat isn't as strong as a full shifter, according to what I understand from my grandmother's warnings, but I still need to have sex."

"That explains the no condoms. And why you smell like me."

"Smell like you?"

Saxon sighed. "She liked to give you bits and pieces of information, huh? Yes, you smell like me. When a female shifter goes into *mating* heat, she takes on the scent of her lover for a time. It warns other males away, especially if she's with child." His eyes traveled down to her stomach and back to her face. "It wears off before the next heat. The male's scent usually lasts a lot longer than a month, but I suppose, with your mixed DNA, your body sheds it faster, which is why I never smelled myself on you when I saw you again."

"That would explain why my grandmother always told me to find a mate or husband as soon as I was old enough." Demi laughed. "She probably never thought I'd be single with different lovers."

Saxon's eyes narrowed.

"It's hard to find someone to date, much less fall in love with and marry, when you're stuck between two worlds," she explained. Not that she cared if he judged her.

"I don't care about that. I just think it's ridiculous that you weren't told everything."

"Yeah, well, she made do, okay? She loved me in her own way, and she thought she was protecting me."

Saxon grinned.

"What's so funny?"

He shook his head. "Nothing." He stood. "I'll be right back."

Saxon left the room, and she closed her eyes. A couple of minutes later, she heard the door open. She sniffed the air, keeping her eyes closed. Two males. Two shifters were with him now. She lifted her lids.

"Demi, this is Vance," Saxon said about the older gentleman. "He's the alpha of the Minnesota Pride."

"Oh. Hello."

Vance smiled and nodded.

"And this is Vaughn, Vance's son, and the next in line to be alpha."

Vaughn looked like a younger Vance.

"Vaughn and I are also both sentinels. We work for Vance, protecting him, his family, and our pride. I explained to them both that you were left in the dark about our kind."

Vance stepped forward. "It's a pleasure to meet you, Demi. Welcome to the Minnesota Pride."

"So, does this mean, you're not going to kill me?"

Vance and Vaughn laughed while Saxon scowled.

Vaughn slapped Saxon on the back. "Great job explaining to her about us, ace."

Saxon pushed his arm away in disgust. "We didn't get that far."

"How long have you known Saxon?" Vance asked her.

"A couple of months." She looked to Saxon, unsure if she should explain their *relationship*. "But we don't know each other that well. We've only…"

Vance patted her hand. "It's okay. You don't have to explain. I can smell him on you."

She felt her cheeks heat.

"I'm just glad you called him when you ran into trouble. We won't let anything bad happen to you."

Demi swallowed. "So, what does that mean for the man who tried to rob us? Did I…"

"Kill him?" Saxon finished for her. "Yes, you did."

"Jesus, Saxon. Tact," Vaughn said.

Demi closed her eyes. She had been afraid of that. "I didn't mean to. I didn't know I would shift like that." She looked up at Vance. "What's going to happen now?"

"We took care of the problem. The police won't be coming after anyone."

She looked at the three men in the room. "Do you have, like, a shifter jail or something?"

Vance laughed. "Or something. But you're not going there either. Didn't Saxon tell you? We know it was self-defense."

Demi crossed her arms—or tried to anyway. That hurt her side, too. "No. He just told me I had a shitty grandmother."

Vaughn laughed loudly.

"I did not," Saxon said.

"I like her," Vaughn said.

Demi smiled. "Thank you."

Saxon growled.

"Down, boy," Vaughn teased him.

"You two, knock it off," Vance said. "Yes, about your grandmother. Once you're feeling better, we need to talk about her."

TWELVE

"SIYA." Someone was shaking her. "Siya, wake up."

Siya blinked her eyes open and looked around before lifting her head. She was still in the waiting room, and she'd fallen asleep on Ram's shoulder. He'd been surprisingly warm and easy to cuddle up to.

"What time is it?" she asked.

"A little after four in the morning."

"That explains why I'm still tired."

"Demi's awake. Do you want to go see her?"

That woke Siya the rest of the way up. "Of course."

Ram grabbed her hand, pulled her from her chair, and led her down a hallway. They stopped at a room, and he knocked on the door.

"Come in," a male voice said on the other side.

They walked in to see Saxon, Vaughn, and Vance, but Siya's eyes were for Demi. She let go of Ram's hand and walked over to her friend.

"How do you feel?" She grabbed Demi's hand. She was too afraid of hurting her to hug her.

"Like I've been stabbed." Demi chuckled.

"I suppose so," Siya said.

"We'll get out of your hair for now," Vance said behind Siya, and she heard footsteps and the door close.

"Are you okay?" Demi asked her.

"Shaken up some but no injuries."

Demi looked Siya up and down. "Where's your shirt?"

"I had to use it to stop your bleeding."

Demi squeezed her hand. "Thanks for your help."

"You're welcome. I bet, now, you're glad I didn't listen to you when you told me to run away," Siya said with a smile.

"Fucking A. But, next time, when someone tells you to run, you listen."

Siya jumped. She hadn't realized Ram was still in the room.

Demi frowned. "Who the hell is that, and why is he trying to boss you around?"

Siya stepped out of her friend's line of sight and saw that Saxon was still in the room, too. She had assumed that everyone had left. "Demi, this is Ram. He was with Saxon when I called." She leaned closer to Demi. "He's a vampire. Did you know that vampires existed?"

"Kind of. I've never met one before though," she said in a normal voice, and Siya shot her a look. "Whispering is futile. I'm pretty sure they can both hear you. Their hearing's better than mine."

"She's right," Saxon said.

Siya crossed her arms over her chest. "Well, that's not fair."

"You never answered why he's bossing you around," Demi said.

Siya shrugged. "He thinks he's in charge of me until this whole situation is resolved."

"There is no think. I am in charge of you and your safety."

Siya looked at Demi and rolled her eyes. Demi laughed, and it was the best sound in the world.

"When do you get out of here?" Siya asked, dropping her arms and grabbing Demi's hand again.

"Later tomorrow," Saxon answered.

"So soon?" Siya asked.

"I think I'll heal just as well at home. Plus, I don't think my insurance will cover this place," Demi joked.

"When do we get to go home?" Siya asked.

"We're going to bring Demi to our place after she's discharged. We need to discuss a few things and make sure there's no trace of what happened. Then, you two are free to go. Ram will take you back to our place today," Saxon said.

Siya thought they were going a little overboard, but she'd never been in a situation like this before.

"Speaking of going home, we'd better go," Ram said. "The sun is going to come up soon."

Siya hadn't even thought about the sun. It was kind of surreal that Ram was a real vampire who had to stay out of the sun.

"Can I hug you?" Siya asked Demi.

"Gently," Saxon said.

"Yes," Demi answered over him.

Siya bent over and wrapped her arms around her friend. "He sure is protective of you."

"I think it's because of his job."

Siya slightly pulled away and furrowed her brow.

"I'll explain later," Demi said. "I'm sorry you can't go home today."

"It's not your fault. It's that guy's fault." Siya stood, letting go of her friend. "I'll be fine." She looked over at Ram, hoping it was true. The whole situation was odd. "Hopefully, they'll give me a bed, so I can get some sleep. That'll kill some time until tomorrow."

Demi took her hand. "I'll see you then."

Siya squeezed. "I'll see you then."

Ram led Siya out of the building and back to her car. She didn't even bother asking if he wanted her to drive. The trip was relatively short as they made their way out of the city and into the suburbs. Soon, Ram was driving up a long driveway. There was a generous-sized house and a slightly smaller house on the same property. The land had to be a couple of acres though, so there was plenty of room.

Ram pulled up next to a group of vehicles, and they exited her car. "This way," he said.

She followed him to the smaller of the two houses, where Ram went straight for the fridge.

"You hungry?"

"I could eat," she said.

"Eggs okay?"

"Yes."

Ram pulled out a carton of eggs, cheese, ham, and a green pepper. "Go ahead and sit."

She took a stool at the counter and watched the man cook. He was making omelets. He had two pans going at the same time. One omelet had six eggs in it, and she wondered who he was making that one for. She also found it amazing that a vampire could cook, but then again, she really knew nothing about them.

"Did you learn to cook in your former life?"

Ram's brow furrowed. "What?"

"Did you learn to cook before you were a vampire?"

Ram grabbed a plate from the cupboard, slid the smaller omelet on it, and pushed it over to her. He took a second plate out and put the bigger omelet on it. He turned off both burners and opened a drawer to get out two forks. He handed one to her and brought the second plate and fork around the counter to her side where he sat down next to her.

He cut off a big bite and shoved it in his mouth.

Siya stared at him.

Ram pointed to her plate. "I thought you were hungry."

"I-I am." She cut off her own bite from her omelet. "How-how are you eating?"

Ram took her free hand and placed it on his chest. His yellow eyes showed a hint of a smile. "Because I'm alive."

She could feel his warmth and his heart beating under her palm.

"I was born a vampire, not turned into one. I need blood to keep me alive, but I also need food." He let her hand go.

"Wow. So, you can have babies? You can get a woman pregnant?"

Ram looked her up and down. "If I wanted to."

His words were laced with heat, and her cheeks grew warm. She was grateful for her dark complexion because it made her red cheeks harder to see.

"You're cute when you blush."

"You can't tell," she protested.

Ram smiled, and she saw a hint of fang. She needed to get a closer look at that later.

"I'm a vampire. I can sense the blood going to your cheeks."

Siya took a bite of her food and swallowed. "I'm beginning to feel less than." It was like being surrounded by superheroes.

"I'll introduce you to Kenzie."

"Who's that?" she asked, a sliver of jealousy coursing through her. She was beginning to feel like Ram was kind of hers and not just until the situation was over.

"She's human, too. She's mated to one of the cat-shifters."

That was nice of him to think of her.

"Thank you. I'd like that."

Ram had cleaned his plate while Siya was only halfway done. He rose from his seat and put his dish in the dishwasher, and then he proceeded to wash the dishes he'd used to make their breakfast.

Who knew a vampire could be so domesticated?

Siya finished her food and put her dish in the dishwasher. "Sorry I didn't help clean up." It was partly a lie. She'd been too tired to make herself get up and help.

"It's fine. Let's go to bed."

She followed him down a hall to where there were several doors.

"Hold on." He walked into a room and came out with a clean T-shirt. He pointed to a door. "There's the bathroom. You can use the shirt as pajamas."

"Is it yours?"

"Yes."

"I'll be right out," she told him. She used the toilet, found stuff to wash her face, and used her finger and toothpaste to brush her teeth. She changed her clothes, leaving on her underwear and the new shirt. It was long enough to be a nightgown.

When she emerged from the bathroom, the hall was clear. "Ram?"

"In here," he said.

She followed his voice to a room. It had two queen-size beds and a half-naked Ram in it. He was barefoot and shirtless. He was quite the male specimen.

"Where is everyone?" she asked. "And why is it so cold in here?" She rubbed her arms.

He shrugged. "Not sure. Reid's probably in his room on the computer. And I run hot." He pointed to one of the beds. "Go ahead and lie down. I'm just going to use the bathroom. I'll be back."

"Is this your room?" she asked.

"Yes. It would be hard for me to keep an eye on you if you weren't here with me."

He had a point. But did that mean she was kicking someone out of their bed?

"Do you have a roommate?"

"No, I have a room to myself," he said as he walked out of the room.

She sighed with relief. It would be weird to sleep in someone else's bed that she didn't even know. She crawled into the bed Ram had pointed to. It smelled of clean sheets and felt incredibly comfortable. She pulled the covers up to her chin, and despite her nap at the infirmary, she closed her eyes, sleep already starting to pull her under.

She heard quiet footsteps come back into the room and felt Ram sit on the bed.

He put his hand on her arm. "Are you already sleeping?"

"Hmm," was all she said in response.

"Good. I'll be right back."

His footsteps left again, and Siya fell further into slumber.

What felt like a million years later, she vaguely felt the bed shift again, and a warmth surrounded her before she finally succumbed completely to sleep.

THIRTEEN

KENDALL AND CAMDEN had gotten home late last night, but her body said it was time to get up.

She kicked off her covers, grabbed clean clothes, and headed to the bathroom. She took a quick shower, dressed, and went to find breakfast.

She was just finishing up her meal when she got a text.

Raven: Heard you had some excitement there last night.

Kendall: Yeah. You guys busy?

Raven: No.

Kendall: I'm heading over. I'll tell you about it when I get there.

No one else was around, so she went to the whiteboard on the fridge and left a note of where she was going. Last she'd heard, there wasn't a meeting until later that night, but if they needed her, they could always call.

It didn't take her too long to drive from the cat-shifters' place to the wolf-shifters', which was nice because she liked to visit often. To her, it was still home, which was kind of ironic because she hadn't lived there that long. Before Damien had become alpha and reunited the wolves and the cats, she and the other sentinels hadn't even lived in the area.

She took a deep breath at all the memories that brought back. She sure was glad that Dwyer wasn't in charge anymore. Damien was ten times the alpha his father had been.

Kendall parked the car and didn't even bother knocking when she entered. Like she'd said, it was still her home.

The first two wolves she saw were Chase and Ranulf.

"Hey, guys," she said as she shut the door.

They were both lounging on opposite ends of the couch, and she couldn't tell if it was early for them or late.

"Hey, Kenny," Chase said. "Come over and sit with us."

Ranulf didn't say anything, but his smile was invitation enough.

Kendall walked over and parked her butt between the two males. "What are you two watching?"

Ranulf shrugged.

"*Daredevil*," Chase said.

"Movie or Netflix show?"

Chase raised his brow like her question was crazy. "Show."

Ranulf sniffed the air. "Your heat coming?"

Kendall slouched down on the couch and crossed her feet at the ankles. "Yeah. I'm hoping I can use Damien and Payton's house for a couple of days, so I can be alone. I really don't want to go to my parents'. It always feels weird to be super horny in their home. Is the alpha here?"

Ranulf pointed to the ceiling. "Listen closely."

Chase hit pause, so the living room went quiet, and

about ten seconds later, there was a faint and distant female moan.

Chase hit play, and Kendall said, "Okay, so I guess I'll wait for them to come downstairs."

Chase elbowed her. "Jealous?" he teased.

"Yes," she admitted even though it had been a joke. "But not that I want Damien for myself." She frowned at the thought. "I just get a little lonely around my heat. It kind of reminds me of what I don't have."

Chase threw his arm around her and pulled her down to his lap as he shoved a pillow under her head. "Hey, if you need some loving, Ranulf and I are here to help."

Kendall looked down at Ranulf to see his reaction, and he patted his legs, so she lifted her feet and set them in his lap. He started massaging her calves, and she studied him. He had light-brown hair and blue-green eyes, and he was the more serious of the two.

She looked up at Chase. He had dark hair and eyes of a cool orange color. Both men were good-looking, and she had heard rumors that they liked to participate in threesomes, but she'd never witnessed evidence of it herself.

"Would this be two separate occasions or one big session?" she asked out of curiosity.

Ranulf gave no indication that he was fazed by her question, and Chase said, "I guess you'll have to say yes to find out."

Kendall snorted. "Knowing my luck, you would both knock me up, and then I'd be tied to not one, but two men for the rest of my life."

"And this would be a bad thing?" Chase asked.

Kendall rolled her eyes.

Chase turned his gaze to Ranulf. "Hey."

Ranulf looked over at him. "What?"

"That should be our next goal."

Ranulf frowned. "What should be?"

"You and me getting the same woman pregnant."

Ranulf rubbed his chin. "Friendship level up?"

"Hell yeah, that's what I'm talking about." He stuck out his fist, and Ranulf bumped it.

"You two aren't serious, are you?" she asked, horrified. "These are children we're talking about."

Chase shook his head and looked to the ceiling. "Jeez, Kenny. Of course we're not serious. Lighten up." He tilted his head toward Ranulf. "Although then our kids would be half-siblings."

"But then they couldn't date each other and mate when they grew up."

"You two are weird," Kendall told them.

They both shrugged.

"Who's weird?" Raven said as she walked into the room.

"These two," Kendall said, pointing at the males.

"I could have told you that."

Kendall sat up and smoothed the back of her hair down. "They offered to help me out with my heat."

Raven's eyebrows rose. "At the same time?"

Kendall shrugged. "I don't know. They won't tell me."

The two females looked at the males, but they ignored them.

The front door opened, and Hunter, the vampire who was living with the wolves, walked in.

"Hey, Hunter," Raven said.

"Hi," Kendall said. She didn't know him well since he'd

come to live with the wolf-shifters when she went to live with the cat-shifters, but she knew him well enough to greet him.

He grunted and took off for the stairs.

"Wow," she said.

Raven lifted her brow. "Yeah, he's been grumpy ever since Quentin left. I think they were better friends than anyone knew."

"That's sad," Kendall said.

"It is," Raven agreed. "When did you get here?" she asked, changing the subject.

"Just a bit ago," she answered.

"Tell me about last night," Raven said as she walked toward the kitchen.

Kendall got up and followed, telling her friend all about Demi and the dead human in the alley as Raven got them both coffee. They sat at the table.

"What's going to happen next?"

Kendall shrugged. "No idea. We're having a meeting tonight."

"So, are things still going okay?" Raven asked.

"Yeah. I miss it here."

Raven nudged Kendall with her foot and smiled. "Hey, if you mate with one of those two boneheads out there, then you can come back."

Kendall took a drink of her coffee. "I think I'll pass."

"I don't blame you."

"I don't know if I could date one of them. Even though they were joking—I think—they're kind of a package. I'd have to take both of them as one." Kendall lowered her voice. "Do you really think they have threesomes?"

Raven smiled and lifted her drink to her mouth. "I have no idea."

Kendall gasped. "You've done it with them."

Raven shook her head, but she was grinning now.

"You have. Admit it."

Raven waved her hands back and forth and started laughing. "I swear, I haven't. At least, not with them."

Kendall gasped again. "You've been holding out on me. What's it like?"

Raven shrugged. "Just like sex with one guy, it depends on who you do it with."

"So, you're saying, it was meh?"

"Yeah, pretty much."

They both started laughing.

"Sucky," Kendall said.

"That's what they kept saying," Raven joked as she gestured to her crotch.

Kendall wrinkled her nose. "Not worth it."

"What's not worth it?" Chase asked as he and Ranulf walked into the kitchen.

"A threesome," Kendall said. "Raven said it was boring."

"She just hasn't had the right men," Chase said as he grabbed two cups from the cupboard and handed one to Ranulf.

Raven rolled her eyes. "Please."

The two males poured themselves coffee and started to head back to the living room.

"With that attitude, I guess you'll never know," Ranulf said as the two left.

"I'm surprised they even have room for a woman with egos that big," Raven said.

"Yeah." She tilted her head. "I'm still curious though."

"I'm not. Please promise me you won't go there."

Kendall laughed. "I promise, I won't. I'll be spending my next mating heat alone and mateless."

She heard more voices in the living room.

"Speaking of my next heat, I have to go and talk to Damien and Payton. I'm hoping I can hang out at their place."

Raven reached over and squeezed her hand. "We won't always have to do it alone."

"I know," she said, but she hoped her friend was right.

FOURTEEN

THE MAN COMES *out of the shadows, and Demi freezes.*

"I'm going to kill you, bitch."

Demi shakes her head. "No. No, you can't. You're already dead."

He sneers and proceeds toward her.

She takes a step back. Or tries to.

Her legs won't move.

The man grins and lifts a knife. "I'm going to make you suffer. Maybe you'll think twice about who you kill next time."

Demi sticks her hands out. "No. Please. I was just defending myself and my friend."

The man begins laughing and raises the knife over his head.

Demi squeezes her eyes shut and screams.

Hands landed down on her upper arms and shook her. "Demi, wake up."

Demi blinked her eyes open, sat up, and lifted her arm to protect herself from the figure in front of her.

"Demi. Hey, it's me."

She slowly lowered her limb. "Saxon?"

He smiled tentatively at her. "Yeah."

She looked around, and her body sagged with relief. "I had...I had a bad dream."

"I could tell." He let go of her biceps. "Do you want to talk about it?"

She shook her head but then began to tell him anyway, "It was the guy...from the alley. He said he was going to make me suffer for killing him."

Saxon ran his hand over her hair. "He can't hurt you any longer."

She looked down at her hands. "I know. It just felt so real."

"They always do."

She looked up. "You have bad dreams, too?"

Saxon smiled. "Yeah." He nodded toward the bed. "Why don't you lie back down and try to get more rest? It's only about seven in the morning, and you still have some healing to do."

Demi pulled the covers up as she lay back down. "I'll try." She looked at the strong male in front of her. It sure helped to know he was there with her, but she'd probably feel better if he—

"Do you want me to lie with you?"

"Do you mind?"

He shook his head. "No. The chair was getting old anyway." He bent over and began unlacing his boots.

"You've been here all night?" she asked, surprised.

"Yep." He didn't bother to look up from what he was doing, as if staying by her side all night were normal.

When he was finished, he stood to pull back the covers

and slipped underneath them, beside her. She was slightly unsure what to do since they'd only spent one whole night together. In the end, she decided that she was injured, and he had offered to lie with her, so she was going to do what she wanted. And that was to lay her head on his chest.

He was warm and smelled so good that she immediately relaxed against him.

Saxon picked up one of her hands and started playing with it. "So, when you shifted, this was the only thing that changed?"

She opened her eyes and moved her head to the bed, so she could see him. "Yeah. I think so anyway. I mean, I couldn't see myself either time, and I wasn't exactly paying attention to my body."

Saxon looked up into her eyes. "How many times have you partially shifted?"

"Twice."

"Once was last night, obviously."

"Yes."

"And when was the other? What were you doing that you weren't paying attention?"

She studied his face to see if he was playing a joke on her, but his expression remained serious. "It was when we were behind the club."

"When behind the club? Was I inside you?"

She swallowed. "Yes." Her voice came out all breathy.

"Was I making you come?"

"Yes," she answered again as she began to grow wet between her legs.

Now was not the time to be thinking about sex. She could barely walk to use the bathroom.

He interlaced their fingers, so their palms were touching. "So, you would say that it happens when you're emotional?"

"I guess so."

"Do you think you can do it again?"

"I don't know. Are you offering to make me come or attack me?"

The corner of Saxon's mouth went up in a half-smile. "Whatever works."

She narrowed her eyes at him. "I can't tell if you're joking or not."

"Have you ever seen another shifter shift?" he asked, leaving her concern unaddressed.

"Just my grandmother."

"Right. Of course. But never your father?"

"No. He passed away when I was little."

"What was it like when you saw your grandmother shift?"

Demi shrugged. "I don't know. At first, I thought it was the coolest thing ever. I was a kid and had never seen anything like it. But, after a while, I began to grow resentful."

"Why?"

"Because I couldn't shift. I was jealous of her, and I was mad at my body. It didn't help that my grandmother pushed me and pushed me."

"When did she pass?"

"When I was seventeen. But she stopped taking me out to the woods to try to shift years before that. She finally gave up, and I did, too."

"Hmm," was all he said.

"Can I see you shift?"

He raised his brow.

"Please?"

Saxon slipped out of the bed and slowly pulled off his clothes. His body was so fluid in its movements, and if she'd just met him, she would think he was trying to turn her on. But it was just how he moved.

Although she was amazed to see his erection when his boxers—his final article of clothing—came off.

"You look surprised," he said, and she guiltily looked up into his eyes. "I can smell your desire, you know."

"Oh." She looked away. She was so used to being around humans; she sometimes forgot that shifters had such a good sense of smell. Even better than hers. "Sorry about that."

Saxon lifted her chin. "Don't do that."

"Don't do what?"

"Apologize. There's no need. You don't need to apologize for who you are or what you're feeling."

"Okay."

Saxon stood back. "Are you ready?"

"Yes."

Saxon shook out his hair and limbs, and in two blinks of her eyes, he was a cat.

"Oh, wow," she said as he jumped onto the bed next to her.

He almost looked like a tiger with his striped hair. Except his fur was brown and blond.

He nudged her hand, so she stroked his head and scratched him behind the ears.

It was the coolest thing she'd seen in a long time. She'd never been allowed to touch her grandmother, much less pet her, so Demi had only experienced this sort of thing with house cats. But Saxon was over ten times bigger.

She touched him everywhere she could, and he let her. She caressed him down his whole back and ran her hand over his tail. She picked up his paws to see how big they were in her palms. And she rubbed her face against his to see how soft he was.

"Can you just stay like this? You'd make the best teddy bear ever."

And, with that, the big cat in front of her became human again.

"I'm not a teddy bear."

She frowned. "You're no fun."

Saxon pulled her sheets over his naked body and put one arm behind his back. "You're not supposed to be having fun. You're supposed to be recovering."

She rolled to her back beside him. "Yeah, I suppose."

"Turn away from me," he told her. "Put your injured side up."

She did as he'd told her and was rewarded with an arm wrapping around her waist.

"I'm here now. You can go back to sleep. No more bad dreams."

And that was exactly what she did.

FIFTEEN

SIYA WOKE SLOWLY from a deep sleep. One of those where you woke up in the same position you'd fallen asleep in. It was the best feeling. Of course, the reason she'd been so tired in the first place wasn't great, but at least today was a new day.

She rolled over and came face-to-face with a sleeping Ram.

She poked his naked shoulder with her finger.

"What?" he said, keeping his eyes closed.

"Why are you in bed with me?"

"I'm keeping you safe." His eyes remained closed.

"And you couldn't do that from the other bed?"

He didn't answer right away, and she realized he'd fallen back asleep. She poked him again.

"What?" he said a little more testily this time.

"Never mind." She sat up and looked around.

The clock on the nightstand said it was after ten in the morning. No wonder she felt great. She hadn't slept that late in a long time. And that meant it was time to get up.

Since she was stuck between the wall and Ram, she threw her leg over him in order to get out of bed.

An eye opened, and he moved to his back.

"Whoa," she said as she grasped his shoulders before she fell off.

"What are you doing?" Ram asked.

She slid off him and onto the floor. "I'm getting up."

He grabbed on to her wrist. "But I'm not. I need you to stay here."

"I'm sure there are others. Besides, I'm not a vampire. I can't sleep all day."

He met her eyes. "You're my responsibility, Siya."

She could feel herself getting riled up. She'd grown up in a culture that viewed a woman as belonging to a man, and she'd worked hard to be her own person and independent. "I'm responsible for myself."

Ram sighed. "I know you are. But you're not in your world; you're in our world. Things are different."

She raised a finger. "Technically, a human was killed, so I think I'm still in my world."

He rubbed his thumb over her wrist. "You bring up a good point. But I was given an order, and I can't just ignore that."

"So, how about we compromise? You see if there is someone else here to protect me, and I'll promise not to leave." At least, not alone. If this place didn't have coffee though, she was going to get some.

Ram smiled. "Compromise. That's a good idea."

She was shocked he'd given in so easily. "It is? I mean, of course, it is."

Ram yanked her closer to him. She stumbled and almost

fell on top of him, so she didn't notice him putting his mouth on the inside of her wrist until he licked her.

Her eyes widened to the point they almost hurt. "What are you doing?"

"Keeping tabs on you," he said and then bit down.

She sucked in her breath and tensed up, but there was only a slight sting where Ram had bitten her. And, after that, she kind of forgot about any possible pain because she was mesmerized as she watched a vampire drink from her.

She could see his cheeks hollow as he sucked, and she could feel his warm tongue on her wrist. It was way hotter than it should be, and she rubbed her legs together to alleviate the new ache she felt in her body.

After less than a minute, Ram licked her wound clean and let her go.

She picked up her arm and studied it. Only two little puncture holes were there, and they were already closed off. They were no longer bleeding.

"Why'd you drink my blood?" she asked and dropped her hand.

"This way, I can feel if you're in trouble."

"Oh." She'd had no idea.

"And, Siya?"

"Yeah?"

He slipped a hand between her legs by her knee and slowly raised it up, higher and higher. When he reached her underwear, he stopped and squeezed the inside of her thigh. "The next time I drink from you, I'm going to do it from here." He closed his eyes and took a deep breath. "You smell fucking amazing."

Does he mean—

94

"Yeah, sweetheart, I mean, your desire. You liked when I drank from you. Who knew? A human." He pulled his hand from between her legs and tapped her on the butt. "Go on. Go eat or whatever it is you need to do."

"Cocky," she muttered under her breath and headed for the door.

"But, Siya?"

She turned. "Yeah?"

"Leave, and I'll know. And I really don't want to get out of bed."

She smiled. "I won't. I promise."

"Good girl," he said and then rolled back over and closed his eyes.

"That's good *woman* to you," she said before leaving the room and shutting the door.

Siya stood in the hall, feeling slightly out of place and hoping she ran into someone friendly.

She walked to the kitchen where a blond man was pouring coffee.

"Good morning," he said with a smile.

"Morning."

"Coffee?" he said, holding up the pot.

"Yes, please."

He grabbed a cup from the cupboard as she took a seat at the counter.

"I'm Camden. I saw you last night, but we didn't really get a chance to meet."

"I'm Siya."

"Nice to meet you, Siya."

☾

Across the hall from Ram's room, Reid was lying in bed, staring at the ceiling.

He'd been up most of the night, and he should be getting some much-needed rest, yet he couldn't shake the feeling that he needed to do something.

"Reid?" his beautiful, naked mate said from his side where she was currently wrapped around him.

"Yeah, Angel?"

"Why aren't you sleeping?"

"I honestly don't know."

Tegan nuzzled his neck with her nose. "I think I can help with your problem."

He smiled. "Oh, yeah?"

She slipped a leg over him and sank down on his cock.

He'd gotten hard the second she said she could help with his problem.

Tegan sat up and began to ride him, her white-blonde hair falling like a veil around her body.

Reid slid a hand up her belly, between her breasts, and up to her neck where he wrapped his hand around her throat. He didn't squeeze; he just held her above him as she rotated her hips over his.

Tegan moaned and clenched around him, and he pulled her down to his mouth.

"You feel amazing, Angel."

She smiled against his lips and pushed her tongue into his mouth.

Reid wrapped his other arm around her waist and encouraged her to ride him harder, faster.

Tegan yanked her mouth from his and panted next to

his ear. Her hands were now in his hair, holding him so tightly that it almost hurt.

Reid quickly flipped them over, so he was on top. Digging his toes into the bed, he began to thrust into his mate as deeply as he could.

Tegan began to whimper, and he knew she was close. He pulled his hand from her throat and replaced it with his mouth. He bit down on her shoulder as she climaxed so hard that she practically sobbed.

He loved when she almost cried when she orgasmed. That his presence, his being inside her, his making her come made her so emotional that she could no longer hold in her feelings. He was one lucky bastard.

Reid slammed into her one more time, letting his own release wash over him as he poured himself into Tegan.

The two of them lay there, limbs entwined, for several minutes while they caught their breaths. Reid slowly rolled to Tegan's side and pulled her into his arms.

She ran her hand over his bare chest. "Hmm…that was great."

He kissed her forehead. "It was," he agreed. He would never tire of making love to her.

Reid rubbed her back until Tegan fell asleep, and he realized that he was not going to be as fortunate. He carefully extracted himself from his mate and slipped out of bed. He pulled on a pair of sweats and parked himself in front of his second love. His computers.

He didn't know what he was looking for, but he had a feeling he would know it when he found it. He checked local news station websites. Nothing unusual. He kept searching and was ready to give up when he found it. And it wasn't good.

He quickly grabbed his cell and called Vance.

"Reid?" Vance answered, his voice raspy. His alpha had probably been sleeping, too.

"Sorry to wake you, but we have a problem."

SIXTEEN

HE HATED THE PLACE. He had only gotten involved with the group when his impressionable, idealistic nineteen-year-old brother, Gavin, became a member. And he hated every second he was there.

PPP was prejudice. They were speciest and sexist, so much so that they had no female members and the wolf-shifters had their own division called Pure Pack Power. Neither group saw the irony in their PPP resembling the KKK, except, instead of keeping different races apart, they wanted to keep different species apart, including subspecies. No one in the group was allowed to be with anyone other than another cat-shifter for any reason whatsoever.

The fact that Eldon had dated a human for three years in high school had been a ding against him. He'd had to fight hard not to roll his eyes that day, instead pretending that he was ashamed of his behavior and was now reformed.

"Eldon," a familiar voice called from behind him.

He spun around to see Gavin running up to meet him. "You got the call to come in, too, huh?"

"I did."

Gavin rubbed his hands together. "I wonder what's going on."

Eldon did his best not to cringe. For whatever reason this impromptu meeting was called, it couldn't be good. Something like that had never happened before, but he had a gut feeling.

The good news was that maybe it would be enough to get his brother to leave this place and never return.

So far, PPP had been a lot of talk and not a lot of action, which was good because Eldon would have hated to see someone hurt. But, with no real threat to society, it was hard to convince his brother to leave.

He'd tried that in the beginning and almost lost Gavin completely.

The two of them entered the main room where other members were sitting around, talking among themselves. Counting Gavin and him, there were thirteen. Unlucky thirteen.

The leader, Donny, was nowhere to be seen, giving Eldon a chance to relax a little. He might not agree with the PPP leader's ethics and views, but the guy was smart and had a strong bullshit meter. It had taken Eldon months for Donny to trust him.

Gavin pulled a chair out at the table, and Eldon took the one next to his brother just as Donny walked in from the back with a laptop in his hand. The man appeared stoic, but there was a little something in his eyes that worried Eldon.

"Good morning, everyone," Donny greeted them,

setting down the computer. "I have something to show you all."

He opened the laptop and turned it around, so the group could see. It was a paused video.

Donny reached over and hit play.

The video showed two women walking and a man approaching them. By their body language—they both went stiff and had horrified looks on their faces—they did not want the man anywhere near them.

There was an exchange between them, and then the man shouted, "I need the goddamn purses! Give them to me now!"

One of the females told the other to run, and she threw herself at the guy.

What in the hell is she doing?

She should have run away with her friend. The two of them fought, and then the unthinkable happened.

The female produced claws and caught the guy in the neck but not before he stabbed the female in the side. The two collapsed on the ground, and the video ended.

"Holy shit," one of the members said. "Who is that?"

"I haven't made a positive ID yet, but I believe this is Demi Cross. She's been on our radar since I was a kid," Donny said. "Her father was a shifter, but her mother is human. It was agreed upon a long time ago that she wasn't a threat to the shifter ways. She was raised almost in secret by her grandmother, and since the older female's death, Demi has lived as a human." Donny rubbed his hands together almost gleefully. "But this," he said, pointing to the computer, "cannot happen again."

Donny stood and began walking around the room. "We

have sat back and watched our future alpha mate with a vampire. We have watched several sentinels mate with others outside their species. And we haven't been able to do a damn thing about it."

Donny stopped and spun toward the group. "But this half-shifter, half-human—this...*abomination*—she is no one special. She is someone we can do something about. We can set an example. And, when we send the message that those relationships and *children* are wrong, others like us—others with the same values we hold—will seek us out, and we will grow."

Donny began pacing again. "And, once we are big enough to protect ourselves, we can let our alpha know—we can let our *community* know—that mating outside the species is forbidden."

Eldon listened in horror as Donny spouted his hate. So far, the leader had been smart enough to not go after the alpha's son or any of the sentinels, but now, Eldon feared the worst. He was afraid that Donny wanted to kill this woman.

"What do you suggest we do?" Gavin asked.

Eldon's head whipped toward his brother.

Gavin looked fierce and ready to fight. It made Eldon sick.

"I'm so glad you asked," Donny said. "First, we need to confirm that this is in fact Demi Cross. I want one of you to go to the restaurant and ask questions."

"I'll do it," George, an older member, volunteered.

Donny nodded. "Good. Make sure to grab one of the uniforms to put on first." Donny smiled up at the ceiling. "My father and grandfather always thought I was silly for buying those police uniforms. Well, look at me now, assholes," he said more to himself than to the group.

Someone cleared their throat.

Donny shook his head and looked down at them. "Yes. I also need a few of you to scout out the hospitals and morgues. We need proof that she injured this man or killed him. And we need to find her. Half-shifter or no, she needed medical help."

A few others raised their hands, including Eldon's brother. It took all his willpower not to shove Gavin's arm down.

"Oh, and, Eldon?" Donny said.

Shit. He was hoping he'd be kept out of it.

"Yes?" Eldon said.

Donny smiled, his expression giving Eldon the creeps. "I need you to use your resources and see if there was a dead body reported or if someone's been arrested."

Eldon had known it was coming, yet it still did nothing to prepare him for how gross he felt, knowing he had to help this dick. Eldon simply nodded.

Donny shook his finger. "You know, I hesitated bringing a Minneapolis police detective into the group even if you are a cat-shifter. But your brother convinced me it was the right thing to do." He lost his smile and leaned forward. "Now's your chance to prove to me your brother was right."

Gavin slapped Eldon on the back. "He won't let us down. Will you, Eldon?"

Eldon looked at his brother. "Nope." Because, in the end, he was going to get Gavin free of them.

He just needed to figure out how.

SEVENTEEN

SAXON'S PHONE rang from the floor of Demi's hospital room.

She mumbled something and went back to sleep.

Saxon slipped out of bed and dug his cell from his pocket. It was Vance.

"Saxon."

"I need you to get Demi out of the hospital and bring her here sooner than planned."

Saxon went on immediate alert. "What's going on?" He grabbed his jeans and pulled them on.

"We have a new development. I don't want to talk about it over the phone. Just find the doctor, get her cleared for discharge, and bring her back here."

"Got it." Saxon hung up and turned to Demi. "Hey, Demi." He ran his hand over her head.

She rolled to her back and smiled at him.

He didn't want to alarm her, so he smiled back. "I'm going to get you up and out of here soon, so I need you to wake up."

"What time is it?"

He looked at his phone. "After ten in the morning."

She frowned. "I thought we weren't leaving until tonight."

He shrugged as if it were no big deal. "Plans change. Vance called and said now is a good time."

"Okay."

Saxon sighed with relief inside. He did not need a freaked-out female on his hands. Or one who asked endless questions. "I'm going to go find the doctor and see if we need to know anything about your aftercare."

Demi slowly sat up and winced.

Guilt ran through him that he was making her leave. "I'll see about getting you some pain meds, too."

She looked around. "Could you see about getting me some clothes, too? I don't think your friends want to see my naked ass."

Saxon growled. "Actually, I think they'd like that too much." And that didn't sit well with him.

Demi laughed and clutched her side. "Ah. Don't make me laugh."

Saxon kissed her on the forehead and smiled. "I'll try not to."

She smiled back. "Thank you."

He headed for the door. "I'll go find your doctor and something for you to wear. Will you be okay until I get back?"

Demi stood, holding on to the bed railing. She let go and held her hands up as if she was testing her balance. "Whew. No dizziness." She looked up at him. "I think I'll be fine. Take your time. I'll just be in the bathroom."

Saxon nodded and left the room.

❨

Saxon led Demi up to a nice-sized home. But, before they entered, he pointed to second building that looked like another house.

"I live over there in the bunkhouse."

She frowned. "Whose place did you take me to those nights I went home with you?"

"That's my place, too. That's where I stay when I'm not on duty and I need to get away."

"I see." She looked at the front door. "So, is this your alpha's house?"

"No."

It isn't?

"This is *our* alpha's home. You're just as much a part of this pride as I am."

She looked down as her face warmed. He didn't realize how much those words affected her. She had always felt like she didn't belong anywhere.

But it was silly to get worked up. She had no idea if everyone felt that way. Her grandmother might have been extreme in some of her thinking, but it didn't mean she wasn't right and that they would want her.

"Come on. Let's get in there," Saxon said, taking her elbow to help her up the stairs.

She could manage on her own, but she was still sore.

The door opened into the living room, which sat empty of people. An older dark blonde woman came from a room at the back of the house, throwing a small towel over her shoulder.

"Hello, Saxon," she said as she came toward them. "You must be Demi."

"That's me."

The female smiled and held her arms out. Demi was completely unprepared for the hug she was given, but she had to admit, it felt nice. Her grandmother hadn't been much for physical affection. Or any kind of affection really. Her mother was a hugger, but she hadn't been around much and had moved out after she remarried when Demi was nine.

The woman let go and stepped back. "I'm sorry," she said with a laugh. "I should probably introduce myself. I'm Lilith, Vance's mate."

"And our alphena," Saxon said with pride.

"Are you hungry, dear?" Lilith asked.

Demi noticed several delicious smells permeating the house.

"Starving," Saxon replied.

Lilith took the towel from her shoulder and smacked Saxon with it. "I was asking Demi." She raised her brow at Demi. "What do you say? Would you like something to eat?"

"Yes, please." Demi hadn't eaten since the night before at the restaurant. They'd been pumping her full of stuff through her IV, but it didn't help the empty feeling in her stomach.

Lilith grinned. "I was hoping you'd say that. I made plenty of food." She stepped off to the side of Demi and Saxon and yelled, "Vance, they're here."

It was so loud that Demi jumped, and Saxon chuckled at her.

An answering, "Okay," was heard from up above them.

Lilith turned back to Demi and Saxon. "Let's head to the kitchen, shall we?"

Demi followed the female into a large kitchen and dining area. There was a huge kitchen island that had several stools pushed under the counter and an enormous dining room table that looked like it'd fit a couple dozen people. But the best part was all the smells and the food sitting on the counter.

Demi could feel her stomach growl. She patted her belly. "I could definitely eat."

"Wonderful," Lilith said. "Why don't you two take a seat? And I'll get some plates."

Saxon guided Demi to the island rather than the dining table, which worked for her. This way, she was closer to the food.

Lilith brought over a couple of plates and forks just as the back door opened, and Vaughn walked in.

He held the door open behind him and whistled. "Hurry up, you two. Grandma's got yum-yums."

Demi snort-laughed at the masculine cat-shifter's use of the word *yum-yums*.

Two little people toddled their way into the house, and Vaughn shut the door behind him.

Demi couldn't stop staring at them. Saxon had told her back at the hospital about all the mixed relationships and that some of the shifters had children. These little cuties were half-vampire. She wasn't the only one who was a mix of two species.

"How're Grandma's little babies?" Lilith asked them with a grin on her face.

"In trouble," Vaughn answered.

"Uh-oh. What did they do?" his mom asked as she picked up the little girl. "What did you do, Victoria?"

Little Victoria giggled as her grandma tickled her belly.

At the same time, the little boy looked around the room and saw her and Saxon. His eyes lit up when they landed on Saxon, and he ran over. To Demi's surprise, Saxon picked him up without any hesitation, set him on his lap, and handed the boy a cookie.

Vaughn sighed and put his hands on his hips. "They got into Naya's makeup and proceeded to paint each other with every single thing they could. We had to throw them in the tub before I got here. I think she was secretly glad the meeting was moved up, so she had the excuse of daylight to stay home."

Lilith smiled. "Every mom deserves a break now and then." She tickled Victoria's belly again. "Right?"

Victoria giggled in response.

"Who's this?" Demi asked Saxon.

"This is Aidan."

Demi shook the little boy's hand. "Nice to meet you, Aidan."

He smiled and hid his face in Saxon's shoulder. The older cat didn't even flinch.

"Are they both Vaughn's?" Demi asked.

"Yeah, they're twins."

"How old?"

Saxon shrugged as he grabbed for some meat and crackers. "One? Two? Beats the hell out of me."

"You don't know?"

He frowned. "No. Why would I?"

He seemed close to the little boy, but what did she know? "Never mind."

"They're sixteen months old," Vaughn said as he walked over and snatched the cookie out of Aidan's hand. "No cookies for naughty boys."

Aidan's lower lip popped out, and his eyes filled with tears. Demi was ready to give him five cookies when Vaughn took a cracker from Saxon's plate and put it in the little boy's hand.

"Eat that."

Aidan studied the cracker and stopped crying.

"That was easy," she said.

"Sometimes, yes." Vaughn picked up another cracker from Saxon's plate and handed it to Victoria.

"*Hey*. Quit taking my food," Saxon said.

Vaughn ignored Saxon's demand, instead asking, "Where is everyone?"

"They should all be here soon."

They all turned to see Vance had walked into the room. His expression was grim, and Demi just knew that whatever he had to say couldn't be good.

EIGHTEEN

DEMI SAT down on the couch between Saxon and Siya, who had been very excited to see her out of the hospital, as Lilith led the twins out of the room.

"Everything going okay?" Demi asked since the two of them hadn't had a chance to really talk yet.

"Yeah. Although I am looking forward to going home. I feel like I'm in an alternate universe."

"Everyone is treating you okay though, right?"

More and more people began to fill the room. Some she had already been introduced to and some she didn't know yet.

"Honestly, I haven't really seen much of anyone. Camden gave me breakfast," she said, pointing to the blond shifter she'd come into the house with. "And Ram gave me a place to sleep." Siya looked around and put her mouth right next to Demi's ear. "He drank my blood this morning when I got up. He said he did it to keep tabs on me. Do you know what that means?" She leaned back to look at Demi.

Demi shook her head. "I don't have much experience with them."

Her grandmother had told her a little about vampires when she was younger. She'd explained that the two didn't get along and that they each stayed on their own sides of the river. But, since Demi acted and lived as a human, she ignored the boundaries. It seemed it was something else her grandmother had been wrong about.

Vance clapped his hands. "Listen up, everyone."

The room quieted.

"Now that you're all here—"

"What about Sawyer and Kenzie?" Saxon asked.

Demi had no idea who he was asking about.

"They can't make it today," Vance said. His eyes darted to Demi. "Next time."

Saxon nodded once.

"As I was saying, I would like you all to meet Demi Cross," Vance said as he pointed at her.

Demi had to fight the urge to slouch in her seat. She hated being the center of attention.

"Demi has been kept a secret from us for over thirty years," he told the group. He turned to her. "Demi, I would like to formally welcome you to the Minnesota Pride."

Everyone clapped, and a few even whistled. Demi's face heated.

"Thank you," she said even though most probably couldn't hear her over their clapping.

After everyone quieted down, Vance asked her, "Do you mind if I share some of your background with the group? Otherwise, we can go talk in private."

Her life was very boring, and the most scandalous thing

about her—her half-shifter/half-human status—was already known to the group. "Share away."

"So, Reid," Vance said, pointing to the redheaded cat-shifter she'd briefly met this morning, who had a laptop open on his knees, "did some digging. Your grandmother, Lucille Harris, was born in 1906 in Minnesota. In 1940, at the age of twenty-four, your grandmother applied for a marriage license with a Floyd Stall."

Demi frowned. "That's not my grandfather's name." Demi had never met her grandfather because he'd died before she was born, but she knew his name was William Cross.

Vance continued, "About a month after they got their license, they were both attacked. Your grandmother suffered from a broken arm and a concussion, but Mr. Stall almost died from being beaten to death. He was in the hospital for three months, and when he was released from the hospital, he promptly moved three hundred miles away. Your grandmother didn't go with him."

"Wow," Demi said. She'd had no idea her grandmother's past was like that. "She never talked about Floyd Stall or being attacked."

Vance smiled in sympathy. "Upon further investigation, we were able to discover that Floyd Stall was human."

Demi's jaw dropped.

"Back then, there was no social media like now to take credit for things, but we suspect that she was attacked by some sort of purity group."

There were a bunch of murmurs among the group.

"What do you mean, purity group?" a female cat-shifter with red-and-black hair asked.

"Just like humans have the KKK, neo-Nazis, and other alt-right groups who believe that people of certain races or religions shouldn't mix, there are shifters who believe the same thing."

"So, why haven't we heard of them before?" Vaughn asked. "And what about Demi herself? Her parents were obviously a shifter and a human. Why did nothing happen to them?"

"I'll circle around to your first question, son," Vance said. "As for Demi, she was born in 1987. Almost fifty years after her grandmother first got engaged. Many things had happened since then. The end of World War II and the end of Nazi Germany, the civil rights movement, and the counterculture movement. Just like humans, shifters became more open-minded as well. Also, Demi's parents never married. There was no record that they were together, like her grandmother's marriage license."

Hearing about her grandmother's past made sense of why she had been overprotective and paranoid. It also explained why she had never been a fan of her father getting her mother pregnant. Demi had always suspected her grandmother was a little prejudiced herself, but instead, she'd probably been worried for her only son.

"So, were these groups only against shifter-human matings?" a male cat-shifter, who had his arm around a pregnant female wolf-shifter, asked.

"From what I learned when I talked to my father, no, they were against interspecies matings of all types. But it seems that humans were sort of the low species on the totem pole." Vance smiled apologetically at Siya.

Siya sighed and said, "Figures," under her breath.

Demi stifled a laugh.

"So, no one has heard of these groups for years?" Vaughn asked.

Vance shook his head. "No. But—"

"So, my grandmother made me scared for nothing," Demi said.

"She was worried about you," Siya said.

"I know. It still sucks." Demi understood it, but it didn't make it any easier, knowing she'd grown up with the rules about her identity pounded into her over and over again. It didn't help, knowing was raised in secret when she didn't have to be.

"All of this could have been explained tonight, like we originally planned," Saxon pointed out. "Why did you move the meeting up?"

Vance looked at Reid, who stood up from the couch and handed his laptop over to the alpha.

"Reid discovered something this morning." Vance hit a few buttons and sighed. "Help me with this."

Reid took the computer back, hit a few more buttons, and gave it back to Vance. "Just hit this," he told the older cat.

"Thank you," Vance said to Reid and looked up at the group of them. "Reid found a video this morning. Of the attack last night, Demi."

Demi gasped.

Siya's hand flew to her mouth.

"Someone was there, recording a video?" Saxon asked, his jaw clenched.

"Unfortunately, yes."

Saxon motioned toward himself, and Vance gave him the laptop. "You just need to——"

"I know, sir," Saxon said.

Saxon hit play, and Demi leaned in close to watch the video with her hands clenched. The attack, which had seemed to last forever, was over in minutes.

Demi sat back, stunned. "I can totally tell that's me." She looked at Saxon. "I'm going to go to jail. Or worse, get locked up and experimented on if they figure out it wasn't a weapon I used to kill that man."

Siya put her hand on Demi's shoulder. "Hey. It only looks like you because you know it's you. The video isn't that great. It was dark, and there was hardly any light in that alley."

Demi smiled at her friend. "Thanks."

Saxon shook his head. "I can't believe he just stood there and filmed it," he said, staring at the screen. His head flung up. "Please tell me we're doing something about this."

"Yes," Reid said. "So far, every video that is popping up is being taken down immediately, thanks to a program I have. Thankfully, the guy has a YouTube channel, so that's the only place he's been trying to post it. Apparently, he makes money off of stuff like this. But, if he goes to another website, my program will find it."

"Why didn't you find it last night?" Saxon said accusingly.

Demi put her hand on his leg. She wasn't sure if it was the right move, but she felt like she had to try to calm him.

But Reid was a big boy and could take care of himself. "Because it wasn't online last night." His voice was firm. "I probably found this within an hour of it being posted. I hauled my ass out of bed for this after being up all night."

Saxon didn't say anything.

"That's what I thought. You're welcome. I also have the guy's address…"

There was a heavy pause.

"Thank you," Saxon mumbled. "Now, can I have it, please?"

"That's up to Vance."

Saxon narrowed his eyes.

"I'll give it to you when this meeting is finished," Vance said. "I want you to go over there and erase it from his phone."

"Consider it done," Saxon said. He looked so angry that Demi was almost afraid of him.

"Demi," Reid said, "I want you to know that, so far, I have not found any evidence that any police have downloaded the video. You have to remember, there is a great big world out there with billions of videos. Think of all the things you see online."

Demi took a deep breath. "That is true."

"There is one more thing though."

"More than the video?" Vaughn asked.

"I'm afraid so," Vance said.

"In my search, I discovered that one person had downloaded it. A Donald Wright."

"Who the hell is that?" Saxon asked.

"Upon first glance, he seems to be no one important. He's a cat-shifter, single, no children, and the manager of a hardware store. But I did some more digging, and his father and grandfather were part of a group that is called Pure Pride Power."

"What the fuck is Pure Pride Power?" Saxon asked.

"They're a purity group," Vance said. "You asked why you hadn't heard of them before, and that's because we can't find any record of them for the last couple of decades."

"So, they no longer exist?" Vaughn asked.

"That's the thought," Vance said.

"But a direct descendant of a purity group has a video of Demi, a half-human/half-shifter, killing someone," Saxon said. "That doesn't sit well with me."

"Me either," Vance said.

Same here, Demi thought. *Maybe my grandmother wasn't so paranoid after all.*

NINETEEN

JEFF SCHULTZ HIT the refresh button on his browser and waited for the page to load.

"*Noooooo*," he yelled into the air and slammed his finger down onto the Enter key on his keyboard in frustration.

He'd uploaded the video he'd taken last night for the umpteenth time, only to have it disappear when he hit the refresh button. It didn't matter what site he used; the video was gone.

"I hate you, you piece of shit," he said as he hit upload again and waited for the file to load.

"Are you talking to your computer, the website, or the internet in general?"

Jeff screamed like a little girl and spun around in his chair. Considering he lived alone, hearing another voice in his living room was cause for him to be freaked out.

The sight before him gave him even more reason.

Three huge men stood in front of him with grim faces, but the one in the middle looked like he wanted to murder

Jeff. He had unusual hair that was blond and brown, and his bright green eyes were filled with fire.

Jeff swallowed. "I-I don't have any mo-money, but ta-take whatever you wa-want."

Green Eyes fisted Jeff's T-shirt and pulled him out of his chair. "Do your thing, Reid," he said to the redhead next to him.

Redhead sat down in Jeff's computer chair and started clicking away at his keyboard.

"Hey, you can't do that," Jeff protested, momentarily forgetting it was one against three.

Green Eyes shook Jeff like a rag doll. "Shut your fucking mouth."

Jeff's teeth clacked with the force of his jaw closing.

"Where's your phone?" the dark blond guy standing next to Green Eyes asked.

Jeff shook his head.

Green Eyes punched him in the mouth, and his head almost came off his shoulders, but he remained standing since Green Eyes still had ahold of his shirt.

"Motherfucker," Jeff shouted. "That hurt."

Green Eyes looked unimpressed. "It was supposed to, asshole. Now, answer the man. Where's your fucking phone?"

Jeff had no idea why these guys were here, and while he'd told them to take anything they wanted, he'd meant anything but his phone. He pursed his lips tight. He didn't care if he got beat up. His phone was his bread and butter.

Green Eyes grabbed on to Jeff's shirt and spun the two of them, so his back was to Blondie. "Search him."

Blondie began patting down Jeff's chest and moved

down. He started with the back of his jeans and came around to his front pockets.

"Oh, I think I've found something," he said when his hand clinically brushed against Jeff's penis.

"Is it the phone?" Green Eyes asked.

"No. Just a tiny penis."

Green Eyes snickered.

"Hey, fuck you," Jeff shouted over his shoulder.

Blondie stood. "I doubt you're fucking much of anything with what you're packing in your pants."

"Packing? Or lacking?" Redhead joked from his seat at the computer without missing a click as he typed away.

"Ha. Good one, Reid," Blondie said.

"Zane," Green Eyes snapped.

"What?"

"Find the phone," Green Eyes said through clenched teeth.

"Chill, man. I'm on it."

Jeff heard Blondie walk away.

Green Eyes dragged Jeff over to the couch and pushed him into it. He pointed a finger. "Stay if you want to keep what's left of your miniscule package."

Jeff immediately covered his crotch with his hands. "I'm not that small."

Green Eyes snickered again. "Whatever you have to tell yourself, man. You obviously don't have any balls if you leave a woman to be attacked by a man in a dark alley at night."

Jeff's eyes widened with panic. "How the hell did you know—"

"Found it," Blondie said as he walked back into the

room. He held Jeff's phone with his forefinger and thumb at the corner. "It was in the bathroom. I hate to think of what he was doing in there with it." Blondie put his other forefinger and thumb in front of his fly and pretended to jerk what could only be a small dick.

Jeff scowled. "I wasn't masturbating. I was taking a shit."

Blondie grimaced and threw the phone at Jeff, smacking him in the chest. "Gross. As if that's better."

"That hurt," Jeff said, rubbing his sternum.

"Man, you are the biggest pussy," Blondie said, shaking his head.

"Pussy or not, you don't stand around and let females get attacked," Green Eyes said with disgust.

"Whoa, whoa," Blondie said, making the time-out sign. "Isa would argue that that's sexist."

Redhead turned around for the first time. "So would Tegan."

Green Eyes rolled his eyes. "Fine. You shouldn't stand around and let *anyone*, male or female, get attacked. At the very least, you call the police." He leaned down toward Jeff. "What you don't do is record it and upload it on the internet." He picked up Jeff's phone. "Now, unlock the thing."

"No." Jeff didn't know what they would do with his files. He needed them to post online. He lived off the money he made on his YouTube videos. He looked longingly at his laptop. His phone was all he had left.

Green Eyes sighed. "Hold him," he said to Blondie.

Blondie trapped Jeff's shoulders against the couch, and before he could fight back, Green Eyes used Jeff's thumb to open his phone.

"Got it."

Blondie released Jeff.

Jeff lunged at Green Eyes, who swatted him back down as if he were a fly buzzing around his head.

Green Eyes started swiping across Jeff's phone and shaking his head every few seconds.

Jeff's bottom lip hurt from him chewing on it so much. He could only guess what Green Eyes was looking at.

Green Eyes walked over to Redhead and threw the phone on the desk. "Wipe them both."

"Already halfway there," Redhead said as Jeff's screen went black, and it began to restart. The initial Welcome message popped up, telling him that everything he'd saved was gone.

Jeff cried out in despair, but inside, he was playing it cool. What these assholes didn't know was that he could still recover the files on his computer. He watched a couple minutes more while Redhead hit a few buttons on Jeff's phone. He was probably resetting the cell, too.

Jeff just hoped they would hurry up and get out of his apartment, so he could go about fixing everything.

Redhead stood. "Done." He handed Jeff's phone to Green Eyes, who then did the impossible.

Green Eyes broke the cell in half with his bare hands.

Jeff shrieked.

Green Eyes opened the patio door and threw the two pieces over the third-story balcony.

Jeff bolted from his seat after being momentarily stunned.

Blondie quickly pushed Jeff back down.

Redhead closed the laptop and handed it to Green Eyes, who did the same thing he'd done with the phone. Green

Eyes then reached in and pulled out the hard drive. He threw it on the ground and repeatedly jammed the heel of his boot on it. After he was satisfied, he threw all the pieces over the railing, too.

Jeff was crying now, tears streaming down his face. "*Why?*"

Green Eyes narrowed his eyes and walked toward Jeff. "Because you are the equivalent of human scum. You had multiple videos and pictures on there of people in bad situations. You are selfish and deserve to rot in hell. Unfortunately, I've been ordered not to kill you."

Jeff squeaked. He didn't want to die.

"Maybe, next time, you'll think about exploiting human suffering."

"I didn't take all those," Jeff protested.

"Doesn't matter. You took the one last night and did nothing. That was a huge mistake."

"How am I supposed to pay my rent?"

Blondie snorted.

"Get a fucking job," Green Eyes said.

"Or change the content of your YouTube channel," Redhead said.

"But then I'll lose my followers."

Blondie shrugged. "Better than dying."

"He just said he was ordered not to kill me," Jeff said, pointing to Green Eyes.

"It doesn't mean he won't." Blondie raised his brow. "I won't tell. Reid?"

"Tell what? I didn't see anything."

Green Eyes smiled, and Jeff thought he was going to shit his pants.

"Okay, okay. No more videos of people getting beat up or fighting or anything else. I promise."

"And?" Green Eyes said.

Jeff's eyes widened. He didn't know what else he was supposed to say.

Green Eyes smacked Jeff on the side of the head. "Next time someone's in trouble, you're going to call the police or step in to help."

Jeff repeated the words.

Redhead looked at his watch. "Saxon, we'd probably better go."

"Yeah, we're done here," Green Eyes said and clocked Jeff under the chin, knocking him out.

☾

When Jeff woke, he was alone.

He scrambled off the couch and ran to his balcony.

Down in the ground, in the middle of the road, were his phone and computer. Even before the truck ran over them, he already knew there was no way he was getting his stuff back.

TWENTY

"UGH, HOW LONG DID I SLEEP?"

Siya looked up from her phone to see Demi walking out of Saxon's room where she'd been napping. He'd rather insisted on her resting, and Demi hadn't refused, telling Siya how much her friend needed her rest.

"Only about an hour."

Demi sat down on the couch next to her. "What are you doing?"

"Going through e-mails, cleaning some stuff out. Nothing exciting. How are you feeling? How's your wound?"

"I'm good, all things considered." She pulled up the side of her shirt. "How does it look?"

Siya leaned closer and gently pushed on the sides of the stitches. "Good. It's a little swollen, which is to be expected." She looked up to her friend's eyes. "Are you taking any ibuprofen? That'll help with the inflammation."

Demi pulled her shirt down. "I just took some."

"Good." Siya sat back against the couch. "I'm sure you'll be back to your normal self soon."

"I hope so. I hate staying back, feeling helpless, letting the men take care of me."

Siya squeezed Demi's arm. "I know."

Demi's grandmother hadn't been very affectionate, and her mother hadn't been around much, so a part of Demi always felt like she was on her own. Add in her super strength and senses compared to most humans, and the woman was fiercely independent.

Thankfully, she was also wise enough to know that she was in no shape to take anyone on. But then again—

"What are you thinking about?" Demi asked.

"How smart you are for staying back when you know you need to recover."

Demi smiled. "Thank you."

"However, you weren't smart enough to not take that guy on last night."

Demi's smile fell, and she didn't look too impressed with Siya.

"I'm just calling it like it is."

"I still beat him, didn't I?"

"Demi."

"Yeah, yeah, you're right. I won't do anything like that again."

There was a sound from the hall, and Ram walked into the living room. His dark blond hair was wet, and he smelled freshly showered. He smiled when he saw Siya, and she had to fight to look away.

"You must be Demi?" he said. "You weren't conscious last night, but I was with Saxon when Siya called us."

"Ah...you must be Ram." Demi held out her hand.

Ram shook it. "It's nice to meet you. Wish it were under better circumstances."

"Same here." Demi smiled.

"I'm going to go and look for something to eat. You two want anything?"

"No, thank you," Siya and Demi said at the same time.

"We already ate," Siya added. "Mrs. Llewelyn fed us a ton of food."

Ram chuckled. "Yeah, she's good at that."

Once he was in the kitchen, Demi smacked Siya on the leg.

He's hot, she mouthed since the open-floor layout would carry anything she said right to Ram's ears.

Siya shrugged.

Demi shook her head and rolled her eyes.

"So, Ram"—Demi raised her voice—"do you have a girlfriend? A mate? Anything?"

Ram looked over his shoulder from his search of the fridge. "I hope not, or I'll be in trouble for sleeping next to Siya today." He looked away.

"What?" Demi said in a loud whisper.

Siya shrugged again. "I'll tell you later. It's not a big deal."

"But—"

The door to the bunkhouse opened, and a couple with an infant car seat walked through the door.

"Hey, Ram," the thin blonde female said.

"Hey, Kenzie. Sawyer," Ram said.

"Hey, man," the tawny-haired man responded.

"What's going on?" Ram asked.

The man, Sawyer, set the car seat down and started

unbuckling it. "We missed the meeting earlier, so we're here to play catch-up." He pulled out a tiny baby dressed in white and purple.

"And we were told there was someone here who would like to meet Zoey," the female, Kenzie, said.

She turned and smiled at Siya and Demi staring from the couch. She walked over to Sawyer and held out her hands. Sawyer set the baby in the blonde's arms, and then Kenzie walked over to the couch.

"Which one of you is Demi?"

Demi held up a hand. "That would be me."

"And you must be Siya?" Kenzie asked.

"Yes," Siya answered.

"I'm Kenzie. I'm human," she said to Siya. "We're a rarity around here."

"I've noticed."

Kenzie laughed. "This is my mate, Sawyer." She pointed to the man who had come in with her. "And this," she said, looking down into her arms, "is Zoey, our little girl."

Siya gasped. "Demi, she's just like you."

Demi smiled, but it was a little wobbly. "Is that true?"

Kenzie smiled. "It is. Would you like to hold her?"

"Can I?"

"Of course." Kenzie gently settled Zoey down into Demi's arms.

Siya moved closer to her friend. "Wow. She's so little." She picked up a tiny hand. "I want to hold her when you're done." She looked up at Kenzie. "If that's okay with you?"

"Of course." Kenzie came and sat down next to Siya. "So, how have they been treating you?"

"Fine. Why?" Siya widened her eyes. "Should I be worried?"

Kenzie laughed. "No." She looked at her mate and smiled knowingly. "Let's just say, not everyone welcomed me with open arms when I came around."

Siya looked over at Sawyer. He looked like he wanted to eat Kenzie alive. "Somehow, I get the feeling that things have changed since then."

"You could definitely say that," Kenzie said, her eyes still on her mate.

The door to the bunkhouse opened again, and a beautiful dark-haired woman came through the door, holding hands with Aidan and Victoria.

"Hey, Sawyer. Hey, Ram," she said.

Siya felt a pang of jealousy in her stomach. She knew it was just a chemical reaction, and it would pass. She'd only met Ram the night before, and while she admitted she was attracted to him, it wasn't a big deal. She hardly developed a relationship with every man she was attracted to. Besides, if she had to guess, this would be Vaughn's wife, or mate, since she was holding the hands of Vaughn's children.

Ram bowed slightly. "Hey, Princess."

"Princess?"

"Oh, yeah. Naya's parents are the king and queen of the vampires," Kenzie answered.

Siya hadn't even realized that she'd spoken out loud.

"Wow."

"Is Vaughn here?" Naya asked.

Ram shook his head. "Not yet."

Naya let go of her kids' hands, and they ran into the

living room, straight to the corner where a toy box was located.

"He should be here soon," Sawyer said. "He texted me, saying he was on his way."

"Yeah, me, too," Naya said. She turned toward the couch and began walking toward them. "Hey, ladies. I'm Naya—"

The door opened again, and in walked a dark-haired man with a toddler on his hip. "Hey, Phoenix here yet?"

Naya turned around. "No, but they should be here soon. At least, according to Vaughn's text."

"Yeah, I got the same one from Phoenix." He set the little boy down and swatted his bottom. "Go play."

The little toddler ran past Demi, Kenzie, and Siya with his little arms pumping back and forth until he reached Victoria and Aidan.

"Who's that?" Siya whispered to Kenzie.

"That's Dante. He's the leader of the Guardians. His mate, Phoenix, is a cat-shifter. She went to live with the vampires when Naya and Vaughn mated. That's why Ram lives with the shifters. The shifters and the vampires traded. But, since Sawyer couldn't go with Vaughn and Tegan today to find Donald Wright, they called Phoenix to go."

"Guardians?"

"Oh, the Guardians are the vampire equivalent of the sentinels. But, unlike Vance and Vaughn, the royal family doesn't get involved with the dirty stuff. They sit in their big mansion and let others do the work." Kenzie smiled. "But Naya's different. She gave up her future seat on the throne to her cousin, so she could mate with Vaughn."

"Wow," Demi said from the other side of Siya.

"Yeah. She's amazing."

The door to the bunkhouse opened once again, and in walked Vaughn, Tegan, and a woman with black-and-red hair. Camden and Kendall—Siya remembered the two of them taking the dead body the night before—came in behind those three about five seconds later.

Vaughn grinned the second he saw Naya. "Hey, baby," he told her before pulling her into his arms and kissing her.

The red-and-black-haired woman kissed Dante, so Siya concluded she was Phoenix.

"Hey, Red," he said.

"Hey. Where's Ash?"

Dante pointed to the living room. "Playing."

Demi unexpectedly handed baby Zoey to Siya. "What did you find out?" Demi asked, standing and interrupting everyone's hellos.

Vaughn turned from his mate and put his hands on his hips. "Phoenix, Tegan, and I went to his house, but no one was home when we got there, so we did a search."

"We broke in," Phoenix explained.

"Yeah, that," Vaughn said. "Reid said the house belongs to Donald's mother, but it looks like he lives there. Or he stays there a lot, going by the mess in his room. I'm sure my father will have someone surveil the house to watch for him to come home." He looked at Camden and Kendall. "Did you two have any luck? Was he at work?"

Camden shook his head. "We went to the last place of employment listed. Not only was he not there, but his former boss also said he hasn't worked there in over a month."

Demi fell back down to the couch. "Well, that was anticlimactic. He's just some jobless loser who lives with his mom."

Vaughn smiled sympathetically. "Don't worry. We'll have Reid do some more digging. We'll find this guy and see why he downloaded the video of you."

Siya looked at her friend's face. She hoped so because she hated to think her friend was in trouble.

TWENTY-ONE

"YOU CAN'T GO HOME."

Demi sighed. She appreciated Saxon's worry, but he was overexaggerating.

"Yes, I can." She should have just left after Vaughn and Camden had come back from finding nothing, but she had thought it would be nice of her to tell Saxon good-bye.

Saxon looked around the crowded living room, grabbed Demi's hand, and pulled her down to his room.

Camden was standing in front of an open closet.

"Get out," Saxon commanded.

Camden raised an eyebrow.

Saxon sighed. "Please."

Camden shook his head and left the room.

"There was a time when that kid was scared of me and did everything I said," Saxon said.

"That must have been before he came to his senses," Demi countered. "Plus, he's hardly a kid."

"It's not important. What is important is you staying safe."

"I've considered your concern, but I don't think I have anything to be worried about." Demi held up her arms. "Besides, I think I've proven I can take care of myself."

"But, now, you're injured."

He was kind of right about that.

"And what if something happens to your wound?"

A perfect idea came to her. She walked over and opened the bedroom door. "Siya," she called down the hall.

A few seconds later, Siya came into view. "Yeah?"

"Can I stay at your place tonight?"

Siya shrugged. "Sure."

Demi smiled. "Thank you."

Siya turned, and Demi shut the door.

"See? Now, I won't be home in case this guy finds my address, and I have my own personal nurse to watch over me."

"Siya's a nurse?"

"Yep. And a damn good one, too."

"I still don't like it."

Demi sighed. "I'm thankful for your concern, but, Saxon, you really don't have to be." She studied his face. "I don't really understand why you feel so responsible for me. I'm not your girlfriend or anything."

"Girlfriend? That's such a human term."

She shrugged. "I'm half-human, in case you forgot."

He stepped closer. "I might not be your boyfriend, but in case *you* forgot, I've been inside you."

She sucked in a breath. Oh, she was sure she'd never forget that as long as she lived. She wasn't going to tell him, but Saxon was the best goddamn lay she'd ever had.

Demi put her hands on his chest. "Yes, you've made me

come a few times, but that doesn't mean you have to uproot your life for me."

His chest vibrated under her palms as he growled, and her breathing quickened.

☾

Saxon looked down at Demi's hands touching his chest as her arousal filled the room. He looked up to her face, seeing the determination there that she could take care of herself. She'd brought up some good points, but he didn't like it.

In fact, it pissed him off. And he didn't know why.

And her scent was messing with his head. He wanted to make her come again.

Saxon pushed his fingers into her hair and kissed her.

Demi immediately opened her mouth for him and wrapped her arms around his neck.

He teased her mouth as he spun her around and guided her back toward his bed.

She must have known immediately where this was going because she pulled at the back of his T-shirt until she yanked it off his head.

With their lips separated, he pushed her back onto his bed and reached for her pants. She was still wearing the scrubs she'd worn when leaving the infirmary. He needed to send her home in something better. Something that didn't remind him of her being injured.

He tore the pants in half, and Demi gasped right before her eyes lit up, and she bit her bottom lip as she grinned.

She wasn't wearing any underwear, and Saxon pushed two fingers inside her.

She moaned as her eyes closed, and her head fell back.

"Nice and wet. Just the way I like it." Saxon pulled his hand away and stood. He shucked off his pants. "Take off your shirt."

She didn't fight him, which was good because all her talk about boyfriends and girlfriends had given him an idea. She might not like it, but it would give him peace of mind, and it would give her the freedom she obviously desired.

He lifted his chin toward the head of his bed, and she scooted up to the headboard.

With both of them naked, Saxon stretched his body over hers and took her mouth again. She ran a hand down his back, and the other she used to grab his cock. The scent of her arousal spiked, and he growled into her mouth. He knocked her hand away and pushed inside her body.

Despite her odd half-shifter mating heat being absent, he found that he wanted her just as much.

Demi pulled her lips away. "Fuck me harder."

Saxon grinned. He'd purposely been taking his time. "If I do that, everyone out there is going to know what we're doing in here. Plus, I don't want to hurt you."

"I don't care. I want to feel you."

He grunted. "Fuck." He hooked the leg of her good side under his arm and pressed her knee to her shoulder. "Okay?" he asked.

She nodded.

He drove into her hard, and Demi moaned. His headboard also slammed against the wall. He did it again. He loved watching her reaction.

"More. Give me more," she demanded.

Saxon stopped playing and began thrusting inside her as

deep as he could go and at a rhythm that had her practically vibrating underneath him.

He kissed her mouth again and down to her ear. Testing her, Saxon nipped at Demi's ear. Rather than push him away, she turned her face toward her raised knee, leaving her neck open and bare for Saxon.

He dug his toes into the mattress, giving him the best angle to get Demi off. He watched her face as she moved closer and closer to her orgasm. Occasionally, he dropped kisses on her shoulder and sucked on the skin there.

Her pussy started clenching down on his cock, and Saxon could barely hold himself back any longer. He dragged his teeth over her neck, and Demi came for him so unexpectedly that he almost forgot his plan.

Just in time, he bit down on her as his own climax hit him so hard that he tasted blood in his mouth. It took a minute or so for his senses to straighten, and Saxon unclenched his jaw from Demi's shoulder and slowly withdrew his shaft from her sweet heat, barbs and all.

Demi came again while Saxon only had enough energy to flop down next to her as he waited to catch his breath and for his strength to return to his body.

He ran his hand down her stomach and in between her legs. He pushed his finger into her, coating it with his seed. He painted the inside of each thigh with his semen and his scent. He rolled on his side, getting up on an elbow to get a better angle, and dragged his other hand between her legs until he felt he had gathered enough wetness.

He trailed his fingers over her mound and stomach and up to her breasts. After sucking on each nipple, he brushed his fingertips over the hardened buds. His trail ended when his scent covered each collarbone, and he looked into her eyes.

She lifted her brow. "Marking me, huh? That's the way we're going to play this?"

He shrugged a shoulder. "This way, if Donald Wright finds you, he'll know that he's not messing with just you."

"Maybe you should have all your friends come in here and come on my naked body. That'll really warn Donald off."

Saxon's vision went hazy, and his nostrils flared.

"Whoa, Saxon, it was a joke." Demi's eyes were round. She put her hand on his chest. "I was kidding."

Saxon jumped off the bed. "Yeah, well, it wasn't funny." He went to his dresser and began going through the drawers.

He heard the sound of Demi moving on the bed.

"Damn, I'm bleeding."

Saxon closed his eyes and winced. "Sorry about that."

"It's fine."

There was a sound of a tissue being pulled out of the box. Demi cleared her throat just as Saxon pushed the last drawer closed, and he turned back to her.

"Does this mean I'm your mate?"

He stepped forward and handed her the items of clothing he'd picked out. "You can wear these."

She looked down at her ripped scrub pants. "Thanks."

"And, no, we're not mates." He pointed to his own neck. "No markings."

Demi pulled his T-shirt over her head. "So, you bite my neck and rub your cum all on me while you walk around with nothing on you. Isn't that a little sexist?"

They both pulled pants on. He had given her a pair of nylon shorts with a drawstring that she could tighten since his clothes were too big for her.

"And, now, I'm wearing your clothes."

Saxon grabbed his shirt off the floor. "It's not a sex thing. It's a *you're in danger, and I'm not* thing."

She narrowed her eyes. "Somehow, I don't think you'd let me bite you and rub my female essence all over your naked body."

He was about to tell her, *Damn right*, when he realized that the idea didn't seem so bad to him. "The situation is totally different. I'm a sentinel. I've been trained to take care of myself. You are not. Plus, you are half-human." He looked her up and down. "Besides, your clothes would never fit me," he said dryly.

Demi stomped her foot. "Quit taking what I'm saying so literally. You know what I mean. If the situation were reversed—"

He shook his head. "I'm sorry, but the situation isn't reversed and never will be." He walked past her and put his hand on the doorknob. He turned. "But, if we ran into a male who was in trouble and Phoenix, Tegan, or Kendall did what I just did to you, I would be all for it." He turned the knob and opened the door.

"Would you think less of the man?"

"Not in the slightest. If it meant keeping him alive, I would say, he was pretty damn smart."

Demi followed him into the living room where, upon their arrival, everyone stopped talking and stared at them.

Saxon narrowed his eyes and dared any one of them to say something.

"Come on, Siya. It's time for us to go."

Siya sprang from the couch.

"Thanks, everyone," Demi said.

"Yes, thank you," Siya said. She stopped in front of Ram. "Thank you."

The side of Ram's mouth lifted. "You're welcome."

"Come on, Siya," Demi said from the door.

Siya hurried over, and the two walked out the door.

"You're just going to let her leave?" Camden asked.

"No. I'm going to give her a head start, and then I'm going to follow her ass home." And then he'd talk to his alpha and ensure that Demi had twenty-four-hour protection.

TWENTY-TWO

BING.

Demi picked up her phone from her kitchen counter.

Saxon: You okay?

Demi rolled her eyes, but she couldn't stop the smile from forming on her face.

It had been a week with no sign of the Donald Wright character. She'd taken Monday off of work and taken it easy the rest of the week. Siya had taken Demi's stitches out on Tuesday, and her wound was almost completely healed at this point.

Besides Saxon's daily texts to see if she was okay and still alive, life was back to normal.

Demi: I'm fine. Still.

Demi: Now is when you can admit that I'm right and you're wrong.

Saxon: I'm never wrong.

Demi: Everyone is wrong sometimes.

Saxon: Whatever you say.

Demi began to reply when her phone rang in her hands. It was her mother.

She sighed before answering, "Hey, Mom."

"Hey, Demi."

Demi had never been close to her mother. Even before she'd gotten remarried, she'd hardly ever been around. When Demi was little, she'd thought it was because her mom was working all the time, but now that she was older, she was sure that her mom had been with her now-husband many of those nights. Her mom had pretty much left her grandmother to raise her.

When her grandmother had died, Demi'd had to live with her mom for almost a year until she turned eighteen. It had been awkward. She'd barely known her stepfather, and her two younger half-sisters were practically strangers.

Then, when she'd started going through her awkward monthly heat, she and her mom had had to keep it on the down-low. Her stepfather and sisters had no idea she was a half-shifter. Her mom had been helpful during that time, but Demi had always felt she'd done it more to keep their secret than because her mother loved her.

To this day, they still weren't close, and her mother never called just to chat or check in.

"What can I do for you?" Demi asked.

"I wanted to remind you that Stephanie's birthday party is in a few weeks."

"I know, Mom. I have it on my calendar."

"Oh, good." Her mother cleared her throat. "So, how have you been?"

"Fine."

There was no point in telling her mom what had

happened last week. Demi knew her mother loved her, but it would just feel weird to have her mom worry about her. It was simply easier not to tell her.

"Work is going okay?"

"Yes."

"Good, good."

Awkward silence.

"And how is Dave? The girls?"

How odd was it that she referred to her two sisters as "the girls"? Especially since they were a little older than girls now.

"Good."

Demi looked at her microwave clock. "That's great. Look, Mom, I have to go." Thankfully, it wasn't a full lie. She was having lunch with Siya. Her mom didn't need to know that she still had two hours to go before picking Siya up.

"Okay. We will talk soon."

"Yep. Bye."

"Bye."

Demi quickly hung up, and after the call screen cleared, she went back to her text message. She hit the home button and set down her phone.

She no longer felt like responding to Saxon. Her mother's phone call had sucked the fun mood out of her.

☾

Kendall drummed her fingers against the steering wheel as she watched Demi park down the street and walk into Siya's house. Today was probably her last shift before she took some time off for her heat, and she was ready for a break. But that was probably more to do with how boring Demi duty had become.

Kendall understood Saxon's worry, but no one had seen any signs of anyone following Demi. But, until Donald Wright was found, they would be watching the half-human. Everyone, including Kendall, was hoping it would be soon. One day shortly, Demi was going to figure out that they were watching her to keep her safe, and Demi didn't seem like the type to be okay with being followed even if it was for her protection.

Something to Kendall's left caught her eye, but when she turned her head and looked, she didn't notice anything out of place.

She rolled the window down and sniffed the air. She smelled a cat-shifter somewhere, but that didn't mean anything. Shifters lived on average roads in average neighborhoods all over.

She was about to turn her head back to the right to watch for Demi to come out of Siya's door when something caught the sunlight, and the hair on the back of Kendall's neck stood on end.

She opened her car door and exited the vehicle, not caring now if Demi saw her. Her instincts were telling her that something wasn't right.

Kendall walked toward Siya's front door while keeping an eye out for whatever she'd seen glint in the sun. But it wasn't her sight that alerted her that there was truly trouble.

Demi and Siya walked out of Siya's house and seemed to be walking toward Siya's car parked on the street. Siya didn't have a driveway, and Demi's vehicle was parked further down. Kendall watched Demi and her friend when she heard the sound of a gun being fired. The shot landed behind the two women on Siya's lawn as Kendall sprinted toward them.

Both Demi and Siya looked scared, but neither of them screamed, which Kendall had to give them credit for. They moved closer to Siya's car as more bullets landed behind them.

It seemed odd that every shot the person had made missed the two women, and the shooter never seemed to correct his aim and shoot closer or in front of the women.

As the two ran for Siya's car, something clicked in Kendall's brain.

The shooter wanted them to seek shelter behind the vehicle.

Kendall began waving her arms. "Stay away from the car! Stay away from the car!"

Both Demi and Siya paused when they noticed Kendall, but then another shot was fired, and they hurried forward. Kendall jumped for the two of them just as Siya's car exploded, knocking them away from the blast.

Kendall couldn't see much because of the smoke, and she couldn't hear anything because her ears were ringing, but she could feel movement under each arm, so she knew Demi and Siya were alive.

The rhythmic pounding of large footsteps vibrated on the ground, and Kendall hoped that someone was calling 911 and coming to their aid.

But whoever had approached them yanked her off the ground in a manner that immediately told her he was not there to help. She could just barely make out the scent of male cat-shifter with the chemicals of the blast permeating the air, which meant he was bigger and probably stronger than her.

Kendall fought his grip to see if she'd mistaken his intentions, but his arms only tightened around her. She rammed her head back against his face at the same time she kicked a leg behind her in hopes she'd get a knee.

She barely skimmed his leg, but her head did connect with his, and she felt a rumble in his chest, as he was probably cursing her out. Her ears were still ringing, so she couldn't make out his words.

His grip loosened, and Kendall was almost free of him when he grabbed her again. An arm went around her neck, and try as she might, she couldn't escape.

She fought for what felt like an hour, but it was probably closer to five or ten minutes until unconsciousness consumed her. Her last thought before going under was how badly she had failed her mission.

TWENTY-THREE

DEMI PUSHED the oxygen mask to her face and took a couple of deep breaths from her seat on the back of the ambulance.

The sight of Saxon walking toward her brought her immediate comfort, and she was aware that she shouldn't rely on him to make her feel better. But she could worry about that later. At the moment, she deserved something nice happening to her.

"Ms. Cross?"

"Hmm?" She looked away from Saxon to the detective standing next to her. "I'm sorry. I didn't hear what you said." She pointed to Saxon. "My friend is here."

The detective smiled politely. He was a handsome black man, but his eyes looked tired, and Demi felt bad for not paying attention and making his job harder.

"I understand you've been through a lot." The detective closed his notebook and pulled out a business card from his suit jacket. "We can talk again soon, after you're feeling better." He handed her the card. "In the meantime, if you think of anything, please call me."

"Will do."

"I'll set up an appointment to meet with you soon."

"Okay."

"We'll speak again soon." As the detective stepped away, he nodded to Saxon as he approached. The detective headed over to the second ambulance where Siya was sitting much like Demi.

"What did you tell him?" Saxon asked.

"Not much." Demi looked down at the card in her hand. "He's human, so I just gave him the basics. I told him I had no idea who had done it." She looked over at her friend. "Of course, being that it was Siya's car in front of Siya's house, it looks like Siya's the target."

Saxon followed Demi's gaze to her friend. "Will she say anything?"

"No. Besides, the detective already spoke to Siya once. I think he's just making sure she doesn't remember anything."

"What did you say about Kendall?"

"Just that someone ran up to us to help when the shooting started and pushed us away from the blast. And, when we came to, she was gone." Demi shrugged. "I didn't know what else to say, but I'm afraid that I made her sound guilty."

Saxon sat down beside her and rubbed her back. "You did the right thing."

After Siya's car had blown up, neighbors had come outside to see what had happened. Demi had quickly asked one of them if she could borrow a cell phone to call Saxon.

She hadn't known if she should call from her own, so she'd told the neighbor it was broken.

Saxon had told her and Siya to give as little detail as possible and not tell the cops that they had seen Kendall getting abducted. He'd promised her it was a shifter matter that they would handle, and while she and Siya had gone along with it, Demi had her doubts.

Demi looked at his face. "Are you sure? Because I feel like I should have told them I saw someone kidnap her. Wouldn't more people looking for her be better?"

Saxon shook his head. "They'd only get in the way."

"But they have resources you don't."

"They don't have Reid. Plus, there are shifter police officers and detectives. We can always reach out for their help."

Demi narrowed her eyes. "You don't even know that this was aimed at me. You're just assuming that the Donald Wright guy was behind this."

Saxon dropped his arm. "You're right. We don't *know* that it was him, but we have a pretty good idea that it was. He couldn't blow up your car, so he waited until you were with your friend."

"Oh? And why couldn't he blow up my car?" Demi had a feeling she wasn't going to like his answer.

"Because we've been watching you. Apparently, we should have been watching both of you," Saxon said the words without any hint of shame or embarrassment.

She scoffed, "You have no qualms about spying on me?"

He met her eyes. "Not a one because I was right." He leaned closer to her, putting them nose-to-nose. "If Kendall hadn't been here, what would have happened? You told me she pushed you away from the car. She saved your ass. So, if you think I'm going to apologize for *guarding* you, you're going to be waiting a long fucking time."

His bullheadedness shouldn't be a turn-on.

"Why do I want to fuck you right now?"

The corner of his mouth curved up for a moment. "Because you know I'm right."

She shook her head. "No. I kind of want to punch you for being right."

Saxon trailed his lips over her cheek and kissed her neck. "Then, it's because you remember how good I fuck you," he said against her ear.

While it was true, it was his confidence that made her hot. He was so sure of himself and his actions. That was what made him so attractive to her. But he probably shouldn't know that. It would only inflate his ego.

"You're a pompous ass."

Saxon chuckled and sucked her neck. He nipped at her there before releasing her. "You can tell me all about what a dick I am when I'm inside you tonight."

She backed away, so she could see his face and raised her brow. "Tonight?"

He shook his head. "Let's not play this game. You know you're staying with us for the near future."

He was right. She knew she was in over her head.

"That doesn't mean I'm staying in your bed."

Saxon shrugged and jumped off the rig. "Suit yourself. You can sleep on the couch if you prefer."

It was just like him to pretend he didn't care where she slept. Except, with Saxon, she wasn't sure he was pretending. But she couldn't let him know that she wanted him to want her to stay with him tonight.

"What about Siya?"

Saxon looked at Demi's friend and then back to her. "Nah. She's cute but not my type."

She rolled her eyes. "I mean, is she coming to stay with you—the shifters—too?"

"Of course. We can't let one of our own hurt anyone, including humans."

Demi breathed a sigh of relief. She had been worried about her friend. She didn't want Siya getting hurt because of her.

She set down the oxygen mask she'd still been holding in her hand and stepped down off the ambulance. "Thank you. I don't want anything to happen to her."

Saxon put his arm around her. "Don't worry. We'll keep her safe along with you."

"We should probably go tell her then. Will we be able to pack some stuff?"

"Sure."

They slowly headed over to Siya.

"Can we have our own room?" Demi asked.

Saxon laughed. "I thought we'd already established that you're sleeping with me. Siya can sleep on the other bed in Ram's room. I think he likes taking care of your friend."

"I'm not fucking you with Camden in the room."

Saxon pulled her close. "I'm kicking his ass out. No one is going to see you naked but me." He loosened his hold, so they could both walk easier.

"And we're going to get Kendall back, right?"

Saxon stopped them in the middle of the street and turned Demi toward him. "You're damn right we're going to get Kendall back. Not only are we on this, but so are the wolf-shifters. We won't stop until we find her." His eyes looked so very green in that moment.

"Okay. I just hope she's okay."

"Kendall is a sentinel. She knows how to take care of herself. She won't put up with anything without a fight. I'm not saying you shouldn't worry, but you should also keep that in mind."

Demi nodded. "Okay."

Saxon put his arm around her again and led her toward Siya.

"But I don't know if it's right that we have sex when Kendall is missing." She mostly said it just to see what he would say.

Saxon shrugged. "Whatever you think. I'm not going to force you."

Demi sighed. Sometimes, his confidence was frustrating. She didn't know why, but she wanted him to fight for her.

"That's very adult of you to say," was all she told him. "Some men would argue about sleeping in the same bed but not getting any."

Saxon laughed as they reached Siya. He leaned down to her ear. "I said I wasn't going to force you. I did not say I wouldn't be getting any."

"You're that sure of yourself, huh?" she whispered.

"When it comes to you, I am." Saxon lifted his head and looked at Siya. "Pack a bag. You and Demi are coming with me."

TWENTY-FOUR

ELDON CURSED the driver in front of him for cutting him off when his cell rang.

"Conrad," he answered without looking to see who was calling. He didn't want to risk hitting the dipshit now in front of him.

"Fuck, fuck, shit."

"Gavin?" *What did my brother do now?*

"Eldon, I need you to come to the clubhouse." A loud crash rang in the background.

Eldon sighed. It was Sunday. He'd just finished running all his errands, and now, he just wanted to relax before going to work tomorrow. "Gavin, I'm kind of in the middle of something right now," he lied. "Can we do this later?"

"No. I...I really fucked up. I need your help."

Eldon pulled his phone away from his face. "Mother-fucker," he cursed with his teeth clenched. He didn't care if his brother could hear him. He put the phone back to his mouth. "Okay. I will be there in about twenty minutes."

He hung up the phone, flipped on his blinker, and took

the next exit. After making his next turn to the clubhouse, he turned the radio on.

"There've been reports of shots fired and a car bomb exploding in a quiet neighborhood in a Minneapolis suburb this morning. At this time, law enforcement has no suspects. There is said to be three victims involved, but the identities of the individuals are unknown at the time."

A chill went down Eldon's spine. There was no way his brother could be behind this, yet his gut instinct was telling him that Gavin was responsible.

After Donny had found the video of Demi Cross, the search for information had turned up nothing. No one had seen anything. There were no mysterious deaths or injuries reported. It was as if the incident hadn't happened. Eldon hadn't even turned up anything in the police database. That meant that this Demi had friends in high places.

Vance Llewelyn must have protected Demi and the whole shifter community from finding out that shifters existed and that Demi had killed someone in self-defense. To Eldon, this'd just proven that mixed species weren't a threat to the shifter way of life, but Donny had been furious.

If this attack on the radio was Demi and Gavin was involved, Eldon was sure that Donny was behind it. His brother would never come up with a plan like this on his own.

Of course, Eldon could just be expecting the worst.

As he raced toward the clubhouse, he could only hope his speculation was all wrong.

Kendall woke with a splitting headache and stared up at a water-stained ceiling. She rubbed the back of her head where it hurt the most and encountered a nice-sized bump. She remembered the gunshots, the explosion, and someone picking her up and strangling her until she lost consciousness. But then…

Ah, yes. She'd woken up in the back of a vehicle and gone for the door. The driver must have hit her to knock her out.

She took her time in sitting up on the old and smelly couch she'd been dumped on and looked around.

It appeared to be an office of some sort. Unfortunately, the desk sat empty and free of any computer. She looked to the door and wondered if she was lucky enough that the thing was unlocked.

There were voices coming from the other side of the door, and they were arguing and getting louder. The good news was that her hearing had returned.

She sniffed the air. Her sense of smell wasn't back to normal yet, but it was better than it had been after the bomb because she smelled the remnants of cat-shifters.

The door swung open, and a dark-haired man stepped through. The sight of him made her catch her breath, but she didn't understand why. She'd never seen him before in her life.

"Holy shit. What the hell did you do?" He stepped forward toward Kendall.

"It was smoky. I couldn't see or smell anything. I didn't know she wasn't Demi," a second voice said from outside the door.

"I'm sorry, ma'am. I don't know what happened, but I'm here to take you home."

A younger man stepped in. "You can't do that." He had lighter hair than the dark-haired man, but they looked similar enough that she guessed they were siblings.

She took a deep breath and realized he was also the guy who had brought her here. Kendall jumped up from the couch and lunged for him, but the dark-haired man stopped her, wrapping her in his arms.

"I know you want to kill him, but that won't solve anything. I need to get you out of here before anyone else shows up."

"You can't take her, Eldon. She's my proof that I didn't screw up."

The man holding her—Eldon—laughed, but it sounded like it was more in disbelief. "I think the fact that you brought a wolf-shifter here is proof that you did screw up."

The younger man stepped back until he was out the door. He shook his head. "No. We can trade her for the half-human or something. I can't let you take her."

"*Fuck*," Eldon yelled as he pushed Kendall out of the way and made a beeline for the door.

Unfortunately, it was too late. The door slammed in his face, and she heard the sound of the lock being sprung.

Eldon slammed his fist against the door. "*Gavin*. Gavin, open this door right now!"

"No. I'm calling Donny."

The echo of footsteps retreated, and Eldon turned around. He slammed his head against the door in frustration. "I don't suppose you've found a way to get out of here?"

She shook her head. "I just woke up before you arrived. I don't suppose you have a cell phone in your pocket?"

"I left it in my vehicle." He pushed himself away from the door. "Well then, we'd better figure out what we're going to do because we can't stay here."

The brunette wolf-shifter crossed her arms over her chest. "And why should I trust you? Your brother—he is your brother, I presume—shot at my friends, blew up one of their cars, and kidnapped me."

Eldon forced himself to look up from her chest where her arms pushed her breasts out. Despite the dire situation, his hormones were surging, and he was this close to getting a hard-on. It was not like him.

Yes, the female in front of him was attractive, but she was far from the first pretty woman he'd crossed paths with.

"My name is Eldon Conrad. Yes, that fucking idiot out there is my brother, Gavin." He moved further into the room just in case Gavin was eavesdropping. "He got involved with the wrong group of people, and I've been trying to pull him out for months now."

The female lifted her brow. "I think you've failed."

Eldon laughed and sat down on the couch. "Miserably." He looked up at the female. "But I want you to know I don't condone his actions. I'm a detective with the Minneapolis Police Department, and I just wanted to get my brother free."

"Why didn't you tell your alpha about them?"

"Because, believe it or not, before today, I never saw

them break any laws. It's all been talk. They haven't done anything illegal in the eyes of human or shifter law. I don't know Vance Llewelyn personally, but I don't believe he would break up a group just because of their beliefs because then, where do you draw the line? Freedom of speech and all that."

He tilted his head to the side. "I don't suppose you're going to tell me who you are?"

The female held out her hand. "Kendall Walker. Wolf-shifter sentinel, ambassador to the cat-shifters."

"Ambassador?"

She shrugged. "Not really. It's more like a liaison program. I'm living with the cat-shifters to help build a better bond between our two species and to help us work together."

"That would explain why you're here and not Demi Cross."

"Yeah. I was on protective duty. You're not the only failure in the room."

Eldon smiled and greeted her with a handshake. Static electricity shot up his arm, and his almost hard-on was now official.

He pulled his arm away and shook the feeling out of his hand. "Fuck. I don't know what it is, but I am suddenly…"

"Horny?" Kendall supplied.

"Well…yeah."

"That's because I'm about to go into heat."

"Great. And here I thought, the situation couldn't get any worse."

TWENTY-FIVE

SAXON LED Demi and Siya into the house.

"With us staying here, will we still be able to go to work?" Siya asked.

Saxon mulled it over in his head. "It'll be up to Vance, but I don't see why not. Someone will have to take you back and forth, of course."

"I wonder if this is what prison feels like," Demi commented.

"Probably," Saxon said. If she was going to be sarcastic, he was, too.

"Seeing as it was my lawn that was shot up and my car that exploded, I'm more than happy to stay here. And, since I don't have a vehicle, I'll take any ride that is offered to me."

Demi winced. "I'm sorry. It's my fault you're in this situation. I'm being insensitive."

Siya shrugged. "I get it. After living with your grandmother, you want your freedom. It's understandable."

"Man, she's got you pegged," Saxon said to Demi.

"Yeah, she minored in psychology."

Saxon walked them to the hallway and stopped in front of Ram's room. "You can stay in Ram's room, Siya."

"Isn't that kind of weird?" she asked.

"No. He's in charge of your protection."

"Does he know this?"

Saxon grinned. "He will when he wakes up. But feel free to tell him now."

"I think I'll wait." Siya opened the bedroom door and stepped inside.

Saxon took Demi's hand and led her down to his room. Camden was sitting against his headboard with a book on his lap. He looked up when they entered.

"I'm kicking you out," Saxon told the younger shifter.

"And where am I going to sleep?"

"You can take Kendall's room until she gets back. She has two beds."

"Why don't you take Kendall's room?"

"Because it would be insensitive to have sex in her room when she's been abducted."

"You could just not have sex," Camden offered.

"Or you could just go and stay in there for the time being," Saxon countered. "Don't forget who's been a sentinel longer."

Camden rolled his eyes. "Fine." He set his feet on the floor. "But you owe me."

"Whatever."

Camden took a bag out of his closet and loaded up some clothes and personal items before taking it across the hall.

"You can set your stuff on Camden's bed," Saxon told Demi.

"What if I want to sleep there instead?"

Saxon bit back a smile, keeping his face straight. She'd made several comments like that all day, as if she wasn't going to be spending the night in his bed with her thighs spread for him. "Go for it. You might want to wash the sheets first though. Camden's been known to sweat."

She wrinkled her nose. "Gross."

Saxon laughed, and Camden stuck his head back in the room. "It's all lies." He smiled at Demi. "You're more than welcome to sleep in my bed."

Saxon narrowed his eyes and growled.

Camden laughed and left the room.

Saxon turned to Demi to see she had a huge grin on her face.

"What?"

She shook her head. "Nothing."

He stared her down, but she just laughed.

"Come on," she said. "I need some food. Siya and I never made it to brunch."

☾

Ram woke and rolled over on his bed, immediately sensing two things. The sun was still up, and someone else was in his room with him.

He moved from his bed to look at the usually empty one in his room to see a sleeping Siya there. He'd already known it was her since some of her blood still ran through his body.

He sat next to her and ran his finger down her cheek. She smiled before her eyes slowly opened.

Her body stiffened when she first saw him but relaxed when she must have recognized him. Despite the blackout curtains in his room, there was plenty of light to make out faces.

"What are you doing here?"

She pushed herself into a sitting position and yawned. "Someone shot at Demi and me this morning and blew up my car. And then they kidnapped Kendall."

Ram had to process her words for a second. "Are you fucking serious? How long did I fucking sleep?"

He looked at his clock. He'd only been sleeping for about five hours, not that he needed much more than that.

"Yeah," Siya answered. "Saxon is convinced it was the Donald Wright guy. He's probably right. He thinks that my house and car were targeted because someone was always watching Demi."

"Someone should have been watching you, too."

She shrugged. "Maybe. I mean, they wouldn't have gone after me if I weren't friends with Demi. I'm not the important one in this scenario."

Ram frowned. "That's not true."

Siya laughed. "I'm glad you think so because Saxon said you're in charge of me."

Ram grinned.

"I mean, in charge of my safety," she clarified.

He shrugged. The two things weren't that different in meaning.

"Are you okay with that?" she asked.

"Of course. It's my job. I've had much worse assignments."

"You're going to be bored."

"We'll see."

"Also, Saxon told me that I was supposed to stay in here. Is that okay? Is that weird?"

"Not at all. It'll be easier to keep you safe when you're sleeping." Plus, for some reason he couldn't decipher, he liked having the human around. He didn't usually care much for their species, but he liked this one. "Although, we'll be sleeping opposite times. As much as I'd like to go out in the sun, it drains me of energy."

"You're in luck. I work nights this week at the hospital, but someone else will still need to come and pick me up in the morning since I get off at six thirty. And, next week, I work evenings—two in the afternoon until ten thirty—so you can pick me up from work." She tilted her head. "If we're still here, that is."

"We'll worry about that later. Do you work tonight?"

"Yes. That's why I was trying to get in a nap." She ran her hands through her hair. "It's strange. When I was sleeping, I almost forgot about everything that had happened, but waking up and seeing you brought it all back."

"Maybe you should call into work."

"No. I'd rather keep busy." She smiled. "Besides, now, I have to pay for a new car. I should start picking up overtime."

"Don't you have insurance?"

"Yes, but it'll only pay for so much."

"You know that the cat-shifters will probably cover the rest. This is not something that you brought upon yourself."

She shook her head. "I can't ask them to do that."

She wouldn't have to ask. They would just do it. But she'd find that out for herself.

"I suppose we should get up and see what else I missed today." Ram stood and stretched his muscles.

When he looked back at Siya, she was admiring his chest. He did a few more stretches that weren't needed just to give her more time to watch him. He liked her eyes on him.

She'd just better not look too low, or she would see the erection threatening to escape his boxers now that he'd seen her staring and smelled her arousal.

She didn't realize it yet, but she was going to end up in his bed, and when she did, it was going to be so good.

Something in Ram told him to take it slow with her and not to rush anything, so he was taking his time. With most women, he'd have already fucked them several times. Siya didn't realize how special she was.

Ram turned from her to go to his dresser. He found a T-shirt and clean shorts, which he threw on the bed. Then, he dropped his underwear and kicked them into his dirty-laundry pile in the closet.

Siya made a noise behind him, and he looked over his shoulder.

"You okay?"

She swallowed, and her eyes moved up from his naked ass. "Um...yeah, sure."

He looked down as if he'd just noticed that he didn't have clothes on. "Sorry about that. I'm used to living with shifters. They take their clothes off all the time."

Siya's eyes got impossibly bigger.

Ram laughed. "Not, like, all the time. They just take their clothes off to shift. It's not a nudist event around here or anything." He reached for his towel and wrapped it around his waist.

"That's a good thing. I don't want to lie to my mother any more than I normally have to when she calls me this week."

"So, you're not going to be telling her that you're sleeping in some male's room?"

"There're just some things she doesn't need to know."

TWENTY-SIX

DEMI WAS HALF-ASLEEP WHEN A LARGE, callous hand ran across her abdomen. Saxon pulled her leg behind her and over his and pushed his cock inside her.

They both groaned at his entry into her body.

This was Demi's second morning waking up next to Saxon, and she was amazed at how insatiable he was. But he wasn't the only one. Demi wanted him inside her as much as possible, and that kind of scared her when she let herself think too much about it.

She wouldn't get to wake up like this forever, and she didn't know how long it would last. She wanted to find Kendall and Donald Wright, but she also didn't want her time with Saxon to end.

Saxon kissed and sucked on her neck as he thrust into her from behind. He hadn't bitten her again, and she really wanted him to. If she asked him to, would he read too much into it?

There was only one way to find out.

"Bite me," she commanded.

Saxon lifted his head and paused mid-thrust. "What did you say?"

She looked over her shoulder into his face. Sure, this was one way to scare a guy away, but Saxon wasn't the sticking-around type anyway.

"I want you to bite me while you fuck me." She lifted her brow. "Unless you think you can't handle it."

Saxon, being Saxon, wasn't threatened by her. He drove inside her, and she moaned.

"I'm more worried you can't handle it."

She grinned. "I can handle anything you give me."

"Oh, yeah?" He pulled out, flipped her onto her hands and knees, and covered her body with his own. He pushed inside her again.

"Yeah," she said as firmly as she could while trying not to sound too breathless. She dropped down on her elbows and moaned at the new angle.

Saxon straightened and grabbed on to her hips as he drove inside her over and over again. "What if I told you I wanted to make you mine?"

She arched her back and pushed her ass back toward him as an answer. They were playing a weird game of chicken, but she liked it.

He slapped her butt. "Okay then, what if I did make you mine?"

She moved her hair off her shoulder and bared her neck to him. "I already told you to bite me."

He dropped his body over hers again and continued to thrust. "You did."

"So, are you going to do it or what?" she taunted.

"All in good time." Saxon kissed her spine on her upper

back then and then both shoulder blades.

"God, you are such a tease."

He chuckled and nipped her ear. "I want to take my time fucking you."

He slowed his hips to a snail's pace, and she wanted to scream.

She decided to turn the tables instead.

Demi dropped to her stomach, effectively pulling her off his dick, and rolled to her side. The surprised look on Saxon's face was priceless, and it made it easier for her to hook a leg on his side and shove him onto his back.

She grinned down at him as she whipped a leg over his hips and straddled him.

"What are you doing?" Saxon asked, his face no longer full of shock but amusement.

"Taking matters into my own hands," she told him as she slowly pushed his cock inside her. She closed her eyes and savored the feeling for a moment.

She didn't know if she'd ever tire of feeling Saxon's thick length pushing inside her.

She opened her eyes again and looked down at Saxon's face. The look of heat in his eyes was one she'd never forget.

"What are you thinking?" she asked him.

"Just how much I love knowing that I'm the one who put that look of ecstasy on your face."

"Hmm…" She picked up his hands and pushed them over his head. "Let's see if I can reciprocate."

"I'm ready, baby."

Demi kissed him as she slowly began to rotate her hips. She didn't want to go too fast or hard yet and realized now that Saxon had probably felt the same. She was a hypocrite apparently.

But Saxon didn't complain. He let her ride him the way she wanted, although he did extract his hands from under hers and touched her all over. Her back, her sides, her legs, her face. It was like he couldn't get enough of her.

When her orgasm was close, she couldn't think much more beyond reaching that sexual high. She held on to Saxon as she moaned and breathed into his ear.

He held on to her waist but didn't take control. It was more of an *I'm here if you need me* gesture.

"Come on, Demi. You're so close. I want to feel you explode. Soak my cock with your cum. Mark me this time."

"Oh shit." Demi's hips bucked as if they had a mind of their own at his words, and she bit down on Saxon's neck.

"Fuck yeah, that feels good," he shouted as he gripped her hips, pushing their lower bodies together as close as they could go as his own orgasm ripped through him.

Demi lay on top of Saxon, boneless and weak. She carefully released her teeth from his neck and was a little horrified to realize she tasted blood. She tenderly licked his wound, and it occurred to her that Saxon was bringing out her cat-shifter half.

She buried her nose in his neck but about had a heart attack when a loud rumble sounded from under her ear.

Saxon wrapped his arms around her when her body jolted. "You okay?"

"Are you...purring?"

"I am." He moved his head away from her, so he could see her face. He frowned. "Did you not know that was something cat-shifters could do?"

She shook her head. "I had no idea. My grandmother never did."

Sympathy filled his eyes. "That doesn't seem right."

Demi slid off Saxon to lie on her back beside him. "Yeah. She wasn't a very happy lady. But, after learning some things about her, I can understand why. But still...to live your life with such constant bitterness isn't good for you."

She rolled on her side toward Saxon. "You never talk about your family."

Saxon shrugged. "There's not much to tell. I had a good childhood. My parents love each other, they love me, and I love them."

"Wow, that must have been so hard for you."

Saxon laughed. "My mother can be a little overprotective, but yes, I had it good, growing up."

"Then, why are you a permanent bachelor?"

His brow furrowed. "What makes you say that?"

"I had you pegged the second I saw you."

An eyebrow went up. "Oh, really? Is that why you didn't like me?"

She snorted. "I didn't like you because you were bossing me around, thinking you knew what was best for me."

He shrugged. "Guilty. You looked innocent and in over your head."

"Would you have said something if I were a man?"

"Yes."

"Liar."

Saxon laughed. "It's true. Not only would, I have before."

She narrowed her eyes at him. "You lie."

"Nope. Two kids—they had to be barely eighteen and probably sporting fake IDs—came in one night. I told them to get the fuck out of there. And they did."

"Well, you are pretty scary."

He met her eyes. "I must not be that scary if you went home with me."

She smiled to herself. "I knew you'd give me what I wanted."

"What's that?"

"A good fucking before we went our separate ways. Like I said, I had you pegged. I met you in Club Seduction after all."

Saxon turned toward her. "If you had me pegged so well, then what are you doing, marking me?"

Her eyes traveled to his neck.

She honestly had no idea. But she did know that she'd liked doing it.

TWENTY-SEVEN

"DO you think death is preferable to being sexually aroused twenty-four hours a day?" Kendall asked from her position on the couch.

They were still trapped in the office. She felt miserable. She was hot despite the ceiling fan blowing on her, her vagina ached, and she had the worst cramps. She was lying in her bra and underwear because she could no longer stand to have clothes touching her overly sensitive body. She'd prefer to be naked, but that didn't seem right to do in front of her prison mate.

Actually, she'd prefer to be in her childhood bed, medicated with the air-conditioning on high. When she went through her heat, she always went home to be with her mom. Her dad would leave town, and her mother would help take care of her. She could really use her mommy right now.

"At this moment, I would say yes, but I know it's not going to last, so in the long run, no," Eldon answered from the bathroom.

There was a window that he was trying to open, so they could escape. The problem was, it was one of those bathroom windows that didn't open because it was made out of glass blocks. The ones that were two to three inches thick and installed with silicone caulking. They didn't have any tools in the room besides an old envelope cutter, and even if Eldon did manage to remove the blocks, there were only four of them. Eldon certainly wouldn't fit through the window, and Kendall wasn't sure she would either. Also, Eldon had told her the clubhouse was not on any main roads and had no close neighbors.

They were fucked.

The stupid bathroom was only a half-bath, too. They couldn't even take cold showers to calm their bodies down.

"It must be nice to have such a positive outlook."

She heard Eldon moving in the bathroom before he stomped into her field of view. He grabbed on to his very generous erection in the front of his boxer briefs. He had taken off as much clothing as possible, too.

"Do you think I like walking around with a fucking hard-on all day? And forget trying to sleep. My fucking dick aches like you wouldn't believe." He pursed his lips. "I am just trying to get through this, the same as you."

Kendall scrambled into a sitting position. "I'm sorry. I didn't mean to judge."

Eldon's shoulders slumped, and he came and sat down beside her. "I'm sorry, too."

She shook her head. "It's my fault."

"No, it's Mother Nature's fault. She really fucked with us, didn't she?"

Why did he have to use the word fucked?

174

Kendall stared at Eldon's chest. He was thin but muscular, and his skin was beautifully tan. She supposed he kept in shape partly for the job, and she guessed partly for himself. He seemed like that kind of guy.

A bead of sweat rolled down from his neck and over his sternum and then across his four-pack of abs. She wanted to lick it off him. And then she wanted to pull down his boxers and shove him inside her until his seed filled her. He smelled incredible, and she wanted his scent all over her.

Kendall had never experienced heat with a partner, but her older sister had told her it was the best feeling. Not only was it the sweetest relief, but she also had the best orgasms when she was in heat. Of course, her sister had a nice mate to help accommodate her, and she wasn't trapped with someone she'd met two days ago.

"Please don't look at me like that."

Kendall met Eldon's eyes where they flashed with heat. She licked her lips.

Eldon's chest rumbled.

Neither of them had actually brought up sex. They both had just seemed to come to the understanding that they would suffer through her heat together. When she'd first met him, she hadn't even considered having sex with him while she was in heat. But, now, it didn't seem like such a bad idea.

Eldon looked away. "You know we can't do this, right?"

"What?"

"Have sex." He turned back at her.

"Why not?" she asked, mostly to see what he'd say.

"Because we'd be doing it under duress and because of the hormones raging through our bodies. You don't really want to have sex with me. I'm just a body."

"You don't know that. And, jeez, give yourself more credit."

He laughed. "I only mean that we just met."

"People have one-night stands all the time." She had no idea why she was arguing with him.

"But, if it were me and another male in the room, would you still choose me?" he asked.

"If it were between you and your brother, I'd choose you, hands down."

Eldon laughed again. "Thanks. But, seeing as how he's the one who put us in here, that's not much of a compliment."

She chuckled.

"Look, when we have sex, I want it to be because we, being in our right minds, want to. Not because our bodies are telling us to."

She raised her eyebrows. "Do you realize that you just said *when* we have sex? Not if we have sex."

Eldon shook his head. "Let's just stop talking about sex altogether. Maybe we can play a game or something?"

"Something like Hide the Penis?"

Eldon burst out laughing. He shook his head with a smile. "I don't think you even want to do it. I think you just like playing devil's advocate."

She thought about it. "I'm not opposed to sex, but yes, I think I like arguing because it gives me something to do. Only one of us can work on the bathroom at a time, and I'm feeling bored and worthless."

He held out the letter opener. "Why don't you go and work on it some then?"

She grabbed for the opener, and their hands touched.

Kendall doubled over in pain.

Eldon put his hand on her back. "Are you okay?"

She shoved his arm away. "Don't touch me." She dropped the letter opener to the floor and lay down on her side. "Sorry for snapping at you, but when you touch me, it makes the cramps worse."

"Mother Nature is a real bitch," Eldon said. He picked up the tool from the floor. "You relax. I'm going to go work on the window some more."

Kendall closed her eyes and must have dozed off a little because she almost fell off the couch when there was a pounding at the door.

"Eldon…Eldon…Eldon," a voice taunted in an almost-singsong tone from the other side.

Eldon came out of the bathroom. "It's Donny."

Kendall jumped off the couch. "Donald Wright is on the other side?"

Eldon nodded as he reached the door. "Are you here to let us out?"

After Gavin had locked the two of them in the office, he'd said that he'd contacted Donny, but no one had come to talk to them yet. Donny had been sending his minions to deliver their food. And, since her heat had started, everyone had been staying clear of the building. It did make trying to escape easier, but that was the only good thing about her heat.

Donald Wright laughed. "No way. I decided I'm going to use the wolf-shifter to demand an exchange for Demi Cross."

"There's no way they'll ever do that," Kendall told him.

Donald just laughed. "A full shifter for a halfling? I'm sure we can come to an agreement."

What the fuck is wrong with this guy?

"No, both of you, back away from the door. I'm here to bring you food, but if either of you makes a move, I'll shoot you both."

Kendall and Eldon stepped away.

"You can come in," Eldon said.

The lock clicked, and the door opened. Kendall could see that Donald matched the picture that Reid had shown them, but that was it. He kicked in two bags of fast food while holding a gun in his hand. He quickly slammed the door closed again.

"What about something to drink?" Eldon asked.

"Use the bathroom sink."

Eldon cursed under his breath.

"I'll come back in a few days—once your little mating heat is over, wolf. I'll hopefully have worked out a deal by then."

Kendall clenched her fists.

"Oh, and, Eldon?" Donny said.

"What?" Eldon answered through clenched teeth.

"I can understand the allure to fuck the wolf. She smells incredible. But know, if you do, I'll find out and cut off your dick. And, if you get her pregnant, I will find her and cut her half-cat baby out of her belly."

Eldon ran to the door and slammed his hand against it. *"You sick fuck."*

Donald laughed. "I knew you were never one of us. Your stupid brother thinks you just want to do the right thing, but I know better. You've never believed in our ways."

Eldon didn't reply. He just clenched his jaw so hard that she thought he was going to chip a tooth. He probably knew it was hopeless to try to protest.

"That's what I thought. No fucking the wolf, cat." Donald's footsteps slowly retreated from the door.

"He's a real piece of work."

"Now, you can see why I wanted to get my brother away from here."

Kendall tilted her head to the side. "Is it wrong that, now, I really want to fuck you just because he said we can't?"

Eldon chuckled and picked up the food. "Come on. We might as well eat."

TWENTY-EIGHT

SAXON WALKED Demi to her car after her shift. "How was work?"

"Good. No creepy guys came in and asked about me. *Again*," Demi pointed out.

Saxon smiled. "I'd still rather not take any chances."

"I did get some questions about you though."

"Oh?"

Demi smiled. "My coworkers want to know who the mysterious hot guy is who brings me to work, takes me home, and keeps an eye on me all day."

"And what did you tell them?" Saxon asked when they reached his SUV.

"They, of course, know about what happened at Siya's house, so I told them you're my bodyguard. I said you're a friend who does security stuff on the side, and you're helping me out."

Saxon stepped closer to Demi, pushing her back against the side of the vehicle. "A friend, huh?" He didn't really like the way that sounded.

"Yeah. Then, they asked if some side benefits came with being friends with you. And they said, if we're not sleeping together, they all volunteer as tribute."

"Huh?"

Demi laughed. "Never mind. It's a book thing." She put her arms around his neck. "Basically, they all want to sleep with you." She ran her fingers through his hair. "Does that happen a lot?"

"Does what happen?"

"Do women just want to have sex with you wherever you go?"

Saxon shrugged. "I don't know. I don't really pay attention." He supposed he'd never really had to work to get someone in his bed.

Demi laughed like she couldn't believe he'd just said that. "I guess that makes sense. It's part of your appeal."

He grabbed her hips and pulled her pelvis toward his own. "So, what did you tell them?"

"Tell who?"

"Your coworkers. Did you tell them I come with benefits?" He kissed her shoulder. "Did you tell them how you rode my cock this morning until you came all over it?" He sucked on the skin at her neck. "Did you tell them how you marked me with your teeth, so other females would leave me alone?"

Saxon was surprised at how much he hadn't freaked out about her biting him. Maybe because it provided her with protection. Maybe because she didn't know the full extent of what she was doing. Maybe it was because marks faded over time. Either way, he actually kind of liked it.

Demi turned her head away, giving him more access to

her throat. He wondered if she knew how much she was telling him with her body language. How she was telling him how much she trusted him. Her grandmother must have explained some of that stuff, but then again, the older woman seemed selective in her teachings.

"Why does that make me so hot?"

Saxon gently bit down on her skin. "What?"

"Your words. I want you to fuck me right now."

Saxon smiled. "Here? In the parking lot where you work?"

"Yes. No. That would be stupid. We'd get caught." She rubbed herself against his aching dick. "But I want you. You're messing with my head."

"Ditto," he said and kissed her.

His phone began buzzing in his pocket.

He pulled away. "Hold that thought," he told Demi. He pulled out his cell and answered it, "Saxon."

"You almost home?" It was Vance.

"No, we're just leaving the library." Saxon pulled the keys from his pocket and unlocked the doors. Demi got in while he went around to the driver's side to do the same. "What's going on?"

"We have a new development. Emergency meeting. Come straight home."

Saxon turned the engine over. "We're on our way." He hung up the phone and took off from the parking lot.

"What's going on?" Demi asked.

"Emergency meeting. All Vance said was, there's a new development."

"Oh my God. I hope Kendall's okay."

Saxon glanced at Demi. The blood had drained from her face, and she was wringing her hands.

He put his hand on her thigh. "Let's not assume the worst until we have to. The fact that we're having a meeting means something needs to be, and can be, done."

"You think so?" The look in her eyes was pleading with him to say it was true.

He squeezed her leg in reassurance. "I know so."

By the time they got back home, Vance and Lilith had a full house. Because Kendall was a wolf-shifter, all of them were a part of the search, too. Even if Kendall hadn't been a wolf-shifter, they would have probably shown up. The cats and wolves had come a long way in mending the broken relationship between the two.

Demi fell behind him as they walked up the steps. "Are they going to hate me?" she asked him after he explained why the extra cars were there.

He frowned. "No. Why would they?"

"I'm the reason she was kidnapped." She straightened her spine. "Look, I can handle it. I just want to know what I'm walking into."

His poor Demi. Always feeling like an outsider and that it was her against the world. If Saxon could shake her grandmother, he would. Demi deserved to know that she wasn't alone.

"I'll be honest. I'm sure some are going to attribute her kidnapping to you, but none of them are going to blame you."

"If I had just stayed with you instead of insisting on going home…"

"But would Siya have stayed? Probably not. They still would have found a way to get to you, Demi, whether it was through your friend or another way. The only ones to blame here are the bad guys. You did not make them come after you. They chose to do that all on their own." He took her hand in his. "Come on. Let's go. They're probably waiting for us."

The two of them walked into the living room. A few eyes went to them, but no one gave them dirty looks or stopped talking to stare. Saxon had to admit, he was a little relieved. He'd been pretty confident in his fellow shifters placing the blame where it belonged, but he hadn't been sure until they walked into the room.

Vance clapped his hands, and Damien put his fingers to his mouth and whistled. The room quieted.

"Damien and I both received phone calls today," Vance said. "Kendall is still alive."

"Who called you?" Saxon asked.

"Donald Wright. He's behind it, just like we suspected. But also, his organization, the Pure Pride Power."

"Shit," Vaughn said. "So, the group is still active?"

"Afraid so," Vance said.

"What do they want?" Saxon asked.

"They want to exchange Kendall for Demi."

"No fucking way," Saxon said the same time Demi stepped forward and said, "I'll do it."

"Over my dead body," he told her.

Saxon had just found Demi. There was no way he was giving her up without a fight.

TWENTY-NINE

DEMI STOMPED out of the house with Saxon at her heels. She needed some room to think and to breathe. There were too many people in there.

"Demi, stop."

She turned when she got to the bottom of the stairs. "You have no right to tell me what to do." She poked him in the chest. "If I want to risk my life for someone else, that's my choice."

Saxon put his hand over hers. "I'm sorry."

She tried to slip her hand free.

"Demi, stop."

She ignored him.

"Will you listen to me, please?"

"Will you let go of my hand?"

He released her, which kind of ticked her off. Now, she had to listen to what he had to say.

"Even if I didn't care about you and didn't want to see you hurt, there is no way Vance is going to let you offer yourself up like that."

Demi crossed her arms across her chest. "He's not the boss of me either."

"He kind of is. He's your alpha."

Hearing Saxon say that made her want to cry for some stupid reason. "I'm not a part of your dumb pride."

Saxon sighed and reached for her hand, but she backed away.

"Fine. Have it your way." He leaned down and picked her up in a fireman's hold.

Demi screeched. "*What are you doing?*"

"You might want to be quiet, or there're going to be several dozen eyes watching us from the window."

Demi tried to see if anyone was looking, but she was facing away from the house. "What are you doing?" she asked again but in a much lower tone.

"I'm taking you running." Saxon walked past the house.

"Running?"

"Yes," Saxon said as he walked them past the bunkhouse, too. "You're a shifter. You need to get out and run."

"But I can't shift. However, I can walk on my own."

"If you can walk, you can run. Even on two legs."

"Does that mean, you're going to put me down?"

"Not until we get to our destination."

"Suit yourself, but you're going to have one sore shoulder."

Saxon smacked her ass. "Don't talk about yourself like that."

"*Ow.*" She tried to reach back and rub her sore bum, but it was too hard to do upside down. "I was just stating a fact. I'm not saying I'm fat or anything."

"Oh."

"Jeez." *Jump to conclusions much?* "Now, my butt hurts."

"I'll kiss it and make it better later."

Hmm…

She liked the sound of that. But she didn't want him to know that. "Pass."

"You know, my nose is very close to your crotch, and your pussy says that was a lie."

"Whatever you say, Maury." She moved around, trying to ease the sudden ache between her legs and to try to drain some of the blood that was pooling in her head.

"Will you stop squirming?"

"If you put me down, I wouldn't have to squirm."

"This is probably far enough anyway," Saxon said and dropped her to her feet so fast that she almost fell over. He grabbed her hand to steady her.

She looked around. They were in an open field with the house off in the distance in one direction and a grove of trees in another.

"Vance and Lilith own all this land. You're free to run here."

Demi turned back to Saxon from taking in the view to see him pulling off his T-shirt. "Whoa. What are you doing? We're not having sex right now."

Saxon laughed and shook his head. "I'm getting ready to shift."

"Oh." She watched his shirt and then his pants fall to the ground. "What does it feel like?"

"What does what feel like?"

"Shifting? My grandmother used to say that I needed to force my body to shift. If I willed it and tried hard enough, I could bring out my cat side." She looked down at the ground. "But I never could. No matter how badly I wanted it."

When her grandmother had given up on trying to teach her to shift, that was when Demi knew she'd never belong. She was too human to be a shifter but too much of a shifter to be human.

Saxon put a finger under her chin and lifted it. "I don't feel that way at all. When I shift, I feel like I'm letting myself go. I don't have to force myself to become my cat because a part of me always is." He ran his thumb down her cheek. "Just like your cat is always a part of you. She might never come out and play, but that's okay because she's still in you." He stepped away, and Demi saw that he was completely naked. "Now, let's go run. Give both our cats a chance to be free."

☾

Demi collapsed on the ground with her arms and legs spread. She was hot and exhausted, but she felt a lot better. Saxon had been right.

He came to her side, collapsed on his cat belly, and began to purr. She wished she could run like him as a cat, but she'd still had fun. He was faster than her, but he'd always come back if he got too far ahead of her.

Saxon's purring stopped, and his breathing evened out. He had fallen asleep rather quickly, but she didn't blame him. The sun was warm, and the grass was cool.

Demi closed her eyes and imagined herself shifting, but unlike the times her grandmother had tried to force it upon her, she thought of Saxon's words. She searched her body and mind for her feline side.

She realized now that her grandmother had been sending her mixed signals. She'd wanted Demi to shift but scared her with stories of what would happen if the shifters discovered she was half-human. So, Demi had spent years suppressing that side of herself.

But, now that the shifters knew she existed, she didn't have to be scared anymore. Sure, there was the awful Pure Pride Power, but there were assholes and hate groups everywhere. Demi wasn't an illegal species or some abomination. She was just…herself.

Demi searched the furthest reaches of her mind before she finally found *her*. Her cat.

And her cat's reaction was something along the lines of, *Bitch, what took you so long?*

Demi laughed out loud.

All this time, she'd thought that she was so strong because she'd been pushing her cat away, but now, she discovered that her cat was what had been giving her strength.

I'm sorry, she told her cat.

Her cat shrugged. *Better late than never.*

I suppose.

You know we're not giving up without a fight. You're not turning us over to Donald Wright like some martyr. We're going to work with the other shifters to bring this asshole down.

I know.

Saxon sighed next to her.

You know I consider him mine, right? her cat told Demi.

This news startled her. *No, I didn't.*

You let me mark him. How could you not know?

How would I have known it was you? Demi asked, amazed.

Because I'm a part of you, remember? And, sometimes, you let me come out. Like when you want to mark the sexy male beside you. Or when you have to fight off someone trying to kill you.

It seemed silly now that she thought about it. Her cat had always been there when she needed her.

Thanks for having my back. Demi just needed to work on letting herself connect with her cat, even when she wasn't stressed or aroused.

☾

Demi woke on the cool grass when she felt a shadow fall over her. She opened her eyes to see a human Saxon up on his elbow, grinning down at her.

"What?" She touched the sides of her mouth. "Was I drooling or something?"

His green eyes lit up, and he laughed. "No. You were purring."

Tears immediately filled her eyes, and she blinked them away. "You're joking."

He made an X across his bare chest. "Cross my heart. You were purring, baby."

She felt a tingle inside and realized her cat liked hearing Saxon call her baby.

"I'm still human though?"

Saxon nodded. "Yes. But you know that you don't have to shift into your cat half to be a member of our pride, Demi. It's not a requirement." He leaned closer to her. "Because you do know that you're a part of our pride, right?

Vance is your alpha. I'm your sentinel along with all the others. And we're not going to let anything happen to you. Your life is no less important than Kendall's."

"I know."

Saxon looked shocked. "Really?"

"Yes." She laughed at the look of incredulity on his face. "While you were sleeping, I had a little talk with…myself. I'm not going to risk my life, but I do want to do whatever I can to bring Kendall back. Will you let me do that?"

"It's not up to me, but I'm sure you can work out something with Vance. He's not going to let you take unnecessary risks because you haven't been properly trained, but I'm sure he can understand how you feel."

"Are you going to kiss my butt now, or do we have to get back?"

Saxon laughed and hopped to his feet in a way no human could do. "I'll have to kiss your butt later. We already missed enough of the meeting."

Demi stood and wiped the grass from the back of her pants. "Okay. But, this time, I'm walking."

Saxon smiled. "Deal."

THIRTY

AFTER TAKING a shower and blow-drying her hair, Siya changed into her scrubs and put her long, dark locks up in a ponytail. The bunkhouse was quiet since everyone was over at the main house. Ram had texted her to come over once she was awake. He promised there was good food, which she really shouldn't pass up.

Working the night shift meant the cafeteria was closed, so you either brought food to work or you starved. Sometimes, they ordered out, but even pizza got old after a while.

But she was starting to feel homesick. It was unusual, staying with a bunch of people she didn't know. Everyone was nice to her, but she felt odd and out of place. She felt like she'd hardly even seen Demi lately as she became more involved with Saxon, which only made the loneliness worse.

Siya left the bunkhouse and headed for the main house. As she closed the door behind her, she saw Demi and Saxon walking her way.

Demi waved. "Hey, lady. Getting ready to go to work?"

"Yeah," Siya shouted back. "Soon. I was going to get something to eat first."

When the couple reached her, Saxon said, "I'll meet you in there."

"Okay," Demi said.

She watched Saxon walk away, and Siya studied her friend.

"Something's different about you."

Demi turned to look at Siya. "Me?"

"Yeah. You look so…happy." There was really no other way to describe it.

Demi beamed. "You won't believe what happened."

"What?"

Demi looped her arm with Siya's and started leading her toward the house. "Saxon and I went out running in the field and trees back behind the house. We fell asleep, and when I woke up, Saxon said I was purring."

"Whoa," Siya said as a million thoughts hit her at once.

"I know, right? I have never been that close to my cat before."

A shaky smile was all she could offer Demi, so she hugged her. It suddenly occurred to her that the way Siya felt like an outsider staying at the bunkhouse was probably how Demi had felt her whole life. Demi deserved to feel like she belonged.

Siya now knew how much she had taken Demi's shifter half for granted. Demi acted so human, except for her big appetite and the horny period she went through each month.

"This is amazing," Siya told her friend. "I am so happy

for you." And she was. She just feared that this would be the moment that their friendship started to unravel.

Demi had new friends now. New friends who understood her far more than she ever could.

Demi stepped back. "Hey. Are you crying?"

Siya touched her cheeks, and her fingers came away wet. "Oh, man. I guess I am."

"What's wrong?"

"Nothing."

Demi tilted her head. "Don't try to fool me."

"I think I'm just getting my period. I'm extra emotional. I'm happy for you, but I also want to go home."

"I'm sorry you're stuck here and that we haven't seen each other much."

The two of them started walking again, and Siya fanned her face.

"No, do not be sorry. You didn't ask anyone to come after you or use me to get to you. And it's not the first time we've worked opposite shifts. I'll be on days again."

"Then, what is it? Is it Ram? Has he been awful to you? I thought you kind of liked him." Demi looked around, confusion on her face. "Hey, wait. I saw him at the main house, but the sun is still out."

Siya shook her head. "Yeah, he puts on clothing and wears a hat to hide his skin. Or something similar to that. Did you know that he won't burst into flames?" she asked in an effort to steer the conversation away from her possible feelings for Ram.

"What?" Demi said in sarcastic shock, holding her hand to her chest. "You mean, the movies lied to us?"

Siya laughed. "Yeah. It just drains all his energy, so he

has to feed more often and sleep a ton. It almost makes him sick if he's out in it too long."

Demi bumped her hip into Siya's. "Okay, so it sounds like the two of you talk. He must not be treating you too badly?"

"He's been a perfect gentleman." Almost too much of a gentleman.

After telling her the first night they'd met that they'd have sex someday and then tucking her into his bed and falling asleep beside her, he hadn't made one single move on her, which was probably for the best. He was a vampire, and she was human. It would be hard to make it work.

She didn't know how she'd ever explain to her parents that Ram couldn't go out in the sun much. Ever since they'd moved back to India, they only came to visit about once a year, but they usually came for a whole month. They were bound to notice that Ram's sleeping habits were a little strange.

Ahh.

She shouldn't even be thinking that far ahead. Ram and she were not a couple.

He could at least hit on her and offer himself up as a sexual sacrifice though. If he were a real gentleman, that was what he'd do.

"I need to get laid."

Demi did a double take, and her eyes grew wide. "Okay. I did not expect you to say that."

"I didn't really mean to say it out loud. Sorry."

"Do you mean by Ram?"

Siya shrugged. "Or by anyone. It's been a while, and it's not fair that you're getting all the sex."

"You want to have sex with Saxon? I can probably arrange something."

"As tempting as that sounds, I think I'll pass."

They had reached the house now, and two of them jumped when Saxon stepped out of the shadows. "You're talking about me like I'm a piece of meat."

"Oh, relax. Siya and I were just joking." Demi laughed. "What are you doing out here? I thought you'd be inside."

"Watching out for you. I'm in charge of your safety, remember?" Saxon looked at Siya. "Speaking of safety, what the hell is Ram doing, leaving you alone in the bunkhouse? I thought better of him."

Siya's face heated, but she played it cool. "Oh. Yeah. Ram drinks some of my blood, so he can sense if I'm in trouble."

Demi's mouth dropped open. "He's been drinking your blood? And you never thought to tell me?"

Siya laughed uncomfortably. "Uh…I guess I didn't think it was a big deal."

Demi scoffed. "Oh, it's a big deal all right." She turned to Saxon. "It is a big deal, isn't it? Vampires don't just drink the blood of anyone."

Saxon shrugged. "Ram never really talks about it. But I know another vampire—I won't say who, but I will say it's not Ram—who only drank from the women he had sex with."

Demi raised her arm. "See? Big deal."

Siya shook her head. "I noticed the use of the word *women* in there, as in more than one. It must not be that important. Besides, he's just keeping me safe."

"Does that actually even work?" Demi asked Saxon. "The blood thing?"

"I think so," he answered.

Demi looked at Siya and smiled wickedly.

Siya stepped back. "Oh no." She put her arm up. "Don't even think about it, Demi Marie Cross."

Demi stepped forward. Siya moved back.

"Demi, please don't hurt your friend," Saxon said.

"I'm not."

"She's just going to tickle me to death," Siya explained. "Whenever I had a toy she wanted, that's what she would do." She looked at Demi. "But that was when we were kids," she pointed out.

Demi held up her hands and wiggled her fingers. "You're never too old to tickle," she said gleefully.

Siya screamed and turned around and ran despite knowing that Demi would catch her.

Five seconds later, Demi tackled Siya to the ground and tickled her sides.

Siya laughed, shrieked, and fought to get free.

Five more seconds later, the door to the house burst open, and Ram ran outside. "*Siya*," he shouted.

Demi stopped tickling Siya, and the two of them sat up. Their legs were tangled, and they both had to push hair out of their faces.

"Damn, it worked," Demi said under her breath, amazed.

"I'm okay," Siya told Ram.

Ram walked toward them. "Are you sure? You look like you've been attacked."

"She looks like she was getting hot and heavy with her

friend," a voice said from the porch. He was a dark blonde man that Siya didn't think she'd met yet.

"*Zane*," Saxon chided.

"You should get inside," Siya told Ram as she stood and dusted off her pants. "The sun is still out." It was starting to set, but it wasn't night yet.

Ram grinned. "The sun's worth it if I get to watch the two of you have sex."

A warm feeling traveled through Siya's body. Maybe he was interested in her after all.

"Look what you started," Saxon said to the Zane guy.

"What? He said it, not me." Zane pointed to Ram.

Ram held out his hand to Siya. "Come on. Let's go get you something to eat before I take you to work."

THIRTY-ONE

"OKAY, let's go over the plan one more time," Vance said to the group shifters, both cat and wolf.

"I still don't like that Demi is a part of this," Saxon said with a growl.

Demi put her hand on his arm. "Donald Wright knows who I am and what I look like. You can't fool him into thinking someone else is me."

"I know. But I still don't like it." Saxon looked at Demi. The thought of her getting hurt or killed made his stomach hurt.

"Saxon, focus, please," Vance said. "If you don't think you can handle escorting Demi, then I will have someone else go."

"Over my dead body."

"That's what I'm worried about."

Saxon took a deep, cleansing breath. "You're right. I've always been a professional. Tomorrow is not the time to change that."

"Wow," Demi said. "I can't believe you admitted someone else is right."

Saxon narrowed his eyes at her. Demi just laughed.

"I'm sorry. I know this is serious," she said to Vance.

Vance nodded to her and then said, "Saxon?"

"Demi and I are meeting Donald and Kendall at the local landfill tomorrow at noon."

"I'm still surprised he agreed to meet there," Vaughn said. "He has to know that we're going to bring backup."

When Vance had called to set up the exchange, he'd suggested the landfill. The exchange was only supposed to involve four people, so Vance had picked a place where all wolves and cats could hide with the stench of the landfill covering up their own scents.

"I'm sure he's got his own group of people he's hiding out there," Damien said.

"I know, but it kind of defeats the purpose if both parties are bringing backup. Especially since we hope to leave with both females. He just wants one. If he had picked a location out in the open where no one could hide, he'd be more likely to leave with Demi," Vaughn said.

"That's a good point," Damien said.

"I know it is, little brother."

Damien shot Vaughn a look.

Apparently, Vaughn had taken to teasing Damien about being younger than him and using his status as a brother-in-law against him.

"Be careful. I'm still alpha," Damien said.

Vaughn grinned. "But not mine."

"Okay. How about I sic your sister on you? Payton knows every button to push with you."

"Fine. But I'll have you know that I meant little brother as a term of endearment."

"No, you didn't."

Vaughn grinned again. "You're right. I didn't."

Vance rolled his eyes and sighed.

"Sorry, Dad," Vaughn said, but once his father turned away, Vaughn made a face behind his back.

Demi clapped a hand over her mouth to stop herself from laughing.

Vance looked up at her. "You okay?"

She dropped her arm and cleared her throat. "Yep. Let's do this."

☾

Eldon looked at Kendall lying, curled up in a ball, on the couch and knew he had to do something. Not that he hadn't been trying already, but her heat was going full force, and she was in pain. She was suffering badly.

He wasn't doing too great either. His balls felt like they weighed a million pounds, and his dick ached from being constantly hard. He couldn't stop sweating, and the need to have sex was making him feel crazy.

He'd never been around a female in heat before. It was some serious shit.

He threw down the letter opener in frustration. He'd been chipping away at the old caulking for days now, and at this rate, they'd escape in about a year.

But they didn't have a year.

Donny had come back to tell them that they'd planned an exchange for Demi Cross as soon as

Kendall's heat was over, which was probably going to be soon.

Eldon stalked back into the office and looked around. A wave of hormones hit him and nearly brought him to his knees, but he widened his stance, unwilling to give in.

He went to the small closet and looked inside once again. In the corner was a wooden baseball bat that he had considered using to knock out whoever brought them their meals. But he had been afraid one of them would get shot. He picked up the bat and studied it. He didn't know if it would stand up to the strength of the glass blocks in the window, but he had to try.

Once he was back in the bathroom, he pounded the top of it against the windows. He pounded and pounded and pounded and pounded until he felt like his arms were going to fall off. The thing didn't budge.

In frustration, Eldon started hitting the wall instead. He went a little crazy. As a detective, if he had come upon someone lashing out the way he was, he'd probably call for a psych eval. But he was so frustrated that he couldn't stop.

When he finally did, his breathing was ragged, sweat poured off of him, and his hands were sore. But he noticed something else. He could smell rain. And he could hear it, too.

Eldon leaned down and looked at the spot he'd been hitting with the bat and saw a miracle.

He could see outside.

The hole he'd made in the wall wasn't very big, but he'd gotten a lot further in the few minutes he'd been hitting it with the bat than he'd gotten the last few days with the window.

With a renewed sense of hope, Eldon began working on the drywall to create a space big enough for them to escape.

It wasn't easy, and it didn't happen right away, but as the sun began to set, there was just enough room for a person to squeeze through.

He dropped the bat to the floor and breathed a sigh of relief. Unfortunately, his body took that as a sign that it was time to sleep, but he had to keep going.

He went to the couch and took a deep breath. Touching Kendall was going to be awful for both of them, but getting out of there was more important than comfort.

He picked her up, and she whimpered.

She tried to turn her body to his, so their pelvises lined up. "What are you doing?"

"I'm getting us out of here and getting you home." He carried her to the bathroom. "I apologize, but this isn't going to be easy." He put her feet out the hole and helped her through it.

"Ow," she said.

"I'm sorry."

"Don't be. I'm outside now." Her joy was cut short when she yelped in pain and bent at the waist.

Eldon quickly turned off all the lights so that they wouldn't shine through the hole and then pushed himself through. He got a couple of scrapes and scratches on the way out, but it was worth it to feel the rain on his skin.

"Do you think you can shift?" he asked Kendall. They'd get a lot farther in their animal forms.

She nodded. "Just give me a sec." She stood up straight and squared her shoulders.

She crumpled to the ground and moaned.

"Shit." Eldon got down on his knee. "Are you okay?"

She shook her head. "I can't shift." She cried out and grabbed her middle.

"It's okay. I'll be right back." He went around to the front of the building even though he didn't have much hope. It was empty. His car was gone. "Fuck." He went back around to where Kendall lay on the ground. "We're going to have to walk. But don't worry; I'll carry you."

To where, Eldon had no idea. But, as long as it was away from there, he'd be happy.

THIRTY-TWO

KENDALL TRIED to relax into Eldon, but his touch was like a brand on her skin. And she hated that she couldn't walk on her own. She'd tried a few times, but the cramping in her abdomen always stopped her short. After a few tries, Eldon had insisted on not letting her try anymore.

"We're here," he said.

Kendall looked around but only saw an old, run-down building. "Where's here?"

"It's a closed gas station. We can get dry, and if I remember correctly, it has a pay phone."

"What's a pay phone?"

"It's a —" Eldon started to explain when he realized she was joking. He laughed. "Making jokes. That's good."

They reached the building, and he set her down under the awning. Five feet away, there was indeed a pay phone.

"Five bucks, it doesn't have service," Kendall said.

"I'll take that bet because things like this get overlooked by the city." He picked up the phone, grinned, and held it out to her.

A dial tone had never sounded so beautiful to her.

"Do you have a phone number for me to call?"

Kendall rattled off Vance's cell and closed her eyes. She must have dozed off some because she heard Eldon talking, but it sounded far away.

"You might want to bring females only," Eldon said. "She's in heat."

A pause or two.

"No, sir. I would never."

A minute or so later, Eldon was shaking her awake.

"Are they coming?" she asked.

He smiled. "Yes. They said they'd be here in about an hour."

"Why so long?"

"The clubhouse was far away from the city for a reason."

"So they could kidnap people?"

Eldon chuckled. "More like so no one could find them." He held out his hand. "Do you want to try to get inside while we wait?"

She nodded and took his hand. He helped her stand, and as he pulled his palm away, she noticed blood on her fingers.

She grabbed his hands and flipped them over.

They were bloody and swollen.

"Oh, Eldon."

He looked embarrassed and gently tried to tug his hands away. "It's nothing."

"It's not nothing." She lifted each one to her lips. "You injured yourself for me."

Eldon sucked in a breath. "You probably shouldn't be doing that."

Kendall could smell his arousal through the rain and looked up into his eyes. He had never once tried to take advantage of her heat and sleep with her. He'd worked hard to get them free while she lay, helpless, on the couch.

She knew part of her thoughts were due to the hormones racing through her body, but they were also her rational thoughts.

Before another cramp took her to the ground, Kendall threw her arms around Eldon and kissed him.

One arm wrapped around her waist, and the other cupped the back of her head as he slammed them into the side of the building.

"Are you sure about this?" he asked breathlessly between amazing kisses.

"Yes. Please hurry."

Eldon ripped her panties in half, and suddenly, he was inside her.

Kendall's back arched so far that her head hit the wall. "Oh fuck. Oh my God." She was already super close to climaxing.

"I'm not going to last," Eldon said.

She scratched at his back. "You don't need to. Come inside me. Please."

Eldon drove into her, thrust after thrust, until he exploded inside her.

The second her womb felt his seed, she came in a rush. This was what her body had wanted the last few days, and it was letting her know.

Kendall held on to Eldon, her claws in his back. "Please don't stop. Don't stop. Please don't stop."

Eldon kissed her neck. "I couldn't even if I wanted to."

All their pent-up arousal had now been unleashed as Eldon fucked them both into multiple orgasms. Toward the end of their fucking session, he turned them around so that his back faced the building and slid to the ground.

Kendall lay against him now with him still occasionally jerking inside her. "Are you still coming?"

"Yes. I can't seem to stop."

She leaned back and looked down at her rounded belly. *That could complicate things.* But that was something to worry about later. With everything that had happened to them the last few days, she doubted she'd get pregnant now.

Kendall kissed Eldon's lips, and he opened his eyes.

She smiled. "They're going to be here soon."

He pulled her close and nipped at her shoulder. "I know. I just"—his body convulsed again—"can't help it. I just want to come inside you over and over again. It's crazy."

She laid her head on his shoulder and stroked his arm. "It's the hormones."

"I'm sorry."

"Don't be. My body likes it, too." Every time he came, her womb contracted as it tried to keep his seed inside her.

After several minutes, Eldon said, "I think it's over. My barbs have receded."

Kendall gently moved her body off his and gasped when his cock pulled out of her. She sat down next to him. "That was intense."

Eldon put his hand on her knee. "Are you okay?"

"Are you kidding? This is the best I've felt in a long time. You must have magic cum."

He laughed. "I feel pretty good, too." He tucked his semi-hard penis into his boxer briefs. "I almost forgot what it was like to not be hard all the time. I will never complain about the size of my dick again. That thing was annoying."

Kendall laughed. "As someone who's now had sex with you, you never had anything to complain about."

He grinned. "Thank you." He looked down at her body. "Sorry about your underwear." It now looked more like a loincloth hanging around her waist. "I did tell Vance to bring clothes."

"You did? Smart thinking."

"Yeah, I never thought the first conversation I'd have with my alpha would be me telling him to bring clothes and to tell him a female was in heat." He winced. "And, now, I realize I lied to him."

"About what?"

"I told him I would never take advantage of you. Now, here we sit, covered in each other's scents."

Kendall put her head on his shoulder. "I'm the one who took advantage of you. Vance will understand."

Eldon kissed the top of her head. "I think it was mutual."

Kendall smiled as she closed her eyes and waited to be rescued.

THIRTY-THREE

ONCE THE PHONE call came through that Kendall had escaped, Demi insisted on going with the shifters. Saxon was upset, but she reminded him that she would be surrounded by plenty of sentinels.

Per Eldon's warning about Kendall's heat, the females were going in one vehicle to pick up Kendall, and the males were going in another to pick up Eldon.

Demi put her hands on his chest. "She risked her life to save mine. I need to see that she's okay for myself."

"What if Donald Wright follows Kendall and this Eldon guy to where they're waiting for us?"

"It's raining out. You even said that makes their scents harder to track."

"Fine," Saxon said, obviously not happy.

Demi lifted her brow. "I wasn't asking your permission. I was simply helping you understand where I was coming from."

Sudden applause sounded behind them.

"Tell him, girl," Tegan said.

"I like her," Phoenix commented.

"I can't wait to tell Kendall about this," Raven, a wolf-shifter sentinel, said.

"Whatever," Saxon said and narrowed his eyes at the female sentinels. "You let her get hurt, I will make your life a living hell."

"Come on, Saxon," Vaughn said.

Saxon kissed Demi on the lips and turned and followed Vaughn out the door.

Everyone was following Eldon's directions to the gas station, and then the men were going to have Eldon show them where Donald's clubhouse was.

The women were going to take Kendall home and help her with whatever she needed to get through her heat.

Demi got in an SUV with Tegan, Phoenix, and Raven. Phoenix was behind the wheel, and Raven sat in the back with Demi.

Tegan turned around in her seat as they followed the large SUV in front of them. "I cannot believe Saxon. You are certainly making an impression on him."

Hearing this warmed Demi's heart, but she played it cool. "Oh, really?"

Phoenix looked at Demi through the rearview mirror. "Really. Saxon and I have been friends for some time. I've never even seen him date anyone."

"Yeah, up until now, the female he's been closest to is Phoenix," Tegan said. "I think the only reason he let her in was because he knew Phoenix was made of stone-cold ice."

Phoenix gave Tegan the finger. Tegan ignored it.

"He knew that Phoenix would never want to mate with him and have his babies, so he was safe. But Phoenix surprised us all when she mated Dante and had his baby. Saxon barely escaped her clutches."

Phoenix pushed Tegan, who laughed at her own joke.

Phoenix met Demi's eyes again. "We're close, but it's only ever been friendship. And, now that I'm mated and I have moved out of the bunkhouse, we're not as close as we used to be." She looked at Tegan. "Saxon never had to worry about me wanting him like that."

"So, what about you, Demi?" Tegan asked. "Do you want to?"

"Do I want to what?"

"Mate with Saxon and have his babies."

"Oh." Demi had not been expecting that question. "I don't think that's on the table. Saxon has pretty much confirmed that he's a lifelong bachelor. I think the two of us together right now is just due to extenuating circumstances."

"He doesn't have to let you sleep in his bed," Tegan pointed out. "Saxon is not that nice."

Well, it's not like he's not *getting something out of it*, Demi thought. The two of them had had sex every night and almost every morning, too.

"I guess I'll have to take your word on that."

"You never really answered my question. If it were an option, would you want to be with Saxon?"

Demi felt weird about answering that because she didn't know. She suspected, if she let herself consider it, she'd say yes. But, as long as she told herself that she couldn't have Saxon forever, she would be okay with saying good-bye.

"Tegan, leave her alone," Raven said. "She's obviously uncomfortable."

"Okay, fine." Tegan turned around and faced forward.

Thank you, mouthed Demi to Raven.

No problem, she mouthed back.

As they got to the location they'd been given, two figures stood up. Demi saw Kendall for a moment before the man, presumably Eldon Conrad, moved in front of her in a protective stance.

The SUV the females were in had barely stopped when Raven jumped out, her arms full of the clothes they'd been told to bring. Raven shoved a few articles at Eldon and then pushed him out of the way to hug Kendall.

Demi opened her door and got out of the vehicle, too.

"What are you doing?" Saxon yelled from the other SUV.

"Going to talk to Kendall."

"Demi," he growled. "You're supposed to stay in the vehicle."

She ignored him and kept walking.

"Hey," she said when she reached the three standing at the gas station.

Kendall and Eldon were quickly trying to put on their clothes.

"The guys are waiting for you," she told Eldon.

"That's what I heard."

She held out her hand. "I'm Demi. Thanks for helping Kendall. I owe her my life. And the life of my best friend."

Eldon chuckled and took her hand. "Yeah, I kind of know who you are. I'm Eldon."

"You do?"

"It's a long story. One I'm sure you'll hear about later." Eldon turned around to Kendall. "You going to be okay?"

Demi decided she liked Eldon right away. First, he'd stood in front of Kendall, and now, he was making sure she was okay before he left. The two had obviously bonded.

Kendall smiled reassuringly at him. "I'm more worried about you."

"I'll be fine." Eldon finished pulling on the shirt they'd brought for him and went over to the SUV.

Demi and Raven continued to block Kendall from the road, so she could finish getting dressed.

"Why are both of you practically naked?" Raven asked. "Eldon said nothing happened."

"It was too hot. We were miserable. And then, when Eldon finally got us free, we didn't think to get dressed first. He had to carry me because my heat was so bad."

Raven scrunched up her nose. "You seem okay now."

"Yeah, I think it's over now."

Demi barely noticed Kendall's hand brush over her lower abdomen.

"At the time, I was pretty miserable, but I'm feeling much better now."

"You smell like him," Raven said.

Kendall shrugged. "Yeah, well, we've been locked in a room together for days while I was in heat. Our hormones were going crazy. I'm not surprised."

Raven pulled Kendall into her arms again. "I'm sorry. I'm not trying to pry. I just want to make sure you're okay." Raven released Kendall.

"I'm good. At least, now, I am. I could use a long shower

and a warm bed. Now that the stress of escaping is over and my heat is gone, I'm completely exhausted."

Demi hooked her arm with Kendall's. "Thank you for rescuing me and Siya. And, if that's what you want in repayment, I'll punch anyone in the face who gets in the way of your shower and nap." She tilted her head toward the SUV. "Let's take you home."

THIRTY-FOUR

ELDON FELT like a bug under a microscope as he rode with the group of cat and wolf sentinels to the location of the clubhouse. Despite the rain, he was sure he smelled of Kendall. It took all his energy not to blurt out, *Yes, I had sex with her. Please, don't kill me.*

It was as if all his years of training in working for the Minneapolis Police Department had left him. He hadn't been a rookie for years, but you'd think he'd just come upon his first crime scene.

At least he wasn't naked.

"Thank you for the clothes," he said to the group of males.

"You're welcome," the one next to him said. The guy had blond-and-brown hair. "I'm Saxon."

Eldon put his palm out. "Eldon."

Saxon looked down at Eldon's hand. He wasn't sure if the guy was going to shake it at first, but Saxon slowly raised his arm and shook Eldon's hand.

"Up there is Damien Lowell, driving. Does that ring a bell?"

Eldon nodded slowly. The wolf-shifter alpha. Another slice of guilt ran through him.

"In the passenger seat is Vaughn Llewelyn. I'm sure you know him, too."

"Yes, of course."

Vaughn turned. "My father sends his regards. You'll be meeting him soon."

Eldon almost asked, *I will?* But then it was obvious he would go and speak with his alpha. "Thank you," he said instead.

Saxon pointed his thumb to the third row.

Eldon turned.

"Behind us are Zane, Chase, and Ranulf," Saxon said, each male lifting his arm when his name was spoken.

Eldon waved. "Hello." He caught a mix of both cat-shifter and wolf-shifter but couldn't tell who was who.

"Is Kendall okay?" Damien asked.

Eldon faced forward again. "Yes. She wasn't hurt at all. She was pretty miserable because of her heat though."

"Is that why you two were practically naked?" Vaughn asked.

"Yes. We were both pretty miserable. I couldn't handle my clothes touching me anymore. Same with Kendall. When we escaped, Kendall could barely walk. Our clothes were the last things we thought about."

"It's probably better that way. Less to track you with."

"I wasn't worried about that anyway. One good thing about Kendall's heat was that everyone left us there alone."

"That's such a relief. I was worried they would rape her," Damien said.

"Oh no, those guys are fanatics. They don't believe shifters should mix. Kendall being a wolf saved her." Eldon leaned forward. "It's there. Up that dirt road."

Damien turned the car and slowly drove over the wet and now-muddy road.

"What a shithole," one of the guys from the third seat said.

"Yeah. It's been around awhile, and no one's bothered to fix it up."

Damien parked, and they all exited the vehicle.

"Where did you escape?" Vaughn asked.

"Around back."

Vaughn nodded his head, and Saxon and Zane went to look while he went for the front door.

"Locked," he said after trying the handle.

"Excuse me," Ranulf said as he pulled something out of his pocket. He had a couple of metal objects out and went to work on the lock.

A few seconds later, the lock popped, and the door was opened.

The group headed inside, but Eldon couldn't make himself. "I'm sorry. I can't." The thought of being stuck in there again was too much.

"I'll stay with him," Chase said.

"Fine," Damien said and disappeared through the door.

Eldon leaned against the building and closed his eyes. He was exhausted, but he knew the night was far from over. For one thing, he had to tell them about his brother's role in the whole thing. It wasn't going to be pretty. He knew they needed to bring his brother in along with Donny before morning.

Eldon's thoughts drifted to Kendall and the way she'd felt when he pushed himself inside her. He had never felt anything so sweet. She'd been hot and tight, and she'd given him the best orgasm ever. If only he could be back at the gas station, making love to her again.

"Eldon."

A hand touched his shoulder, and he was startled awake. It was Vaughn.

"Sorry. I think I fell asleep."

"It's fine. You've had a long day." He looked at the club-house. "No one there, just like you predicted." Vaughn looked back at the vehicle where Saxon was throwing something in the back. "They did get your clothes though."

"Thank you."

"I noticed keys in your shorts pocket. But no vehicle."

"Yeah, I'm guessing they took it in case we escaped."

"Who has a key?"

Eldon swallowed.

Vaughn raised an eyebrow.

"My brother."

"Your brother? How is he involved?"

The other sentinels slowly walked up to Vaughn and Eldon.

Eldon took a deep breath. "My brother is the one who shot at Demi Cross and her friend. He's also the one who blew up the car and kidnapped Kendall."

Everyone looked confused.

"I thought Donald Wright was behind all of this."

"Oh, he is," Eldon said. "This is his clubhouse. This is

his club. But my brother was the one who actually carried out the actions that day."

"You know we can't let him get away with this," Vaughn said.

"I know. And I don't want him to. I had hoped my brother could be saved, but now, I know Gavin is beyond redemption."

"We're going to have to brief Vance on this," Damien said.

"Yeah," Vaughn said.

"I think we should go and pick up my brother first," Eldon said.

A few faces looked surprised.

Vaughn clapped him on the back. "I'm glad to hear you're with us."

"He locked me up, too," Eldon said.

"Let's go then," Damien said.

They walked toward the vehicle when Eldon remembered. "What are you going to do about Donny? Donald Wright, I mean."

Vaughn shook his head. "We've been trying to find him for weeks. He's in the wind. Do you think he'll come back here?"

"He's supposed to make the exchange tomorrow, right? He'll be back for that."

Damien shook his head. "Not now that we've spread our scents all over that place. Even with the rain, they're going to know we were inside. All it takes is someone showing up before him and warning him."

"So, what should we do?" Vaughn asked.

"Oh, so now, you want my opinion?"

Vaughn grinned. "Sure do, little brother."

Confused, Eldon watched Damien roll his eyes. Vaughn was a cat, and Damien was a wolf.

"Damien is mated to my little sister," Vaughn told Eldon.

"Ah, that's right. I think I heard about that." It all made sense now.

"Okay. Zane, Chase, and Ranulf, you three stay here. Vaughn, Saxon, Eldon, and I will go to pick up Eldon's brother. We'll call and have Phoenix, Tegan, or Raven bring a vehicle out here. They can help you bring in anyone who comes to the clubhouse."

Vaughn slapped Damien on the back. "I knew you could do it."

Damien pushed Vaughn's hand away. "Fuck you."

Vaughn pretended to think about it. "Nah. I'll leave that to my sister."

☾

Eldon knocked on Gavin's apartment door.

"One second," his brother shouted from the other side.

Footsteps sounded from inside, and Eldon didn't even bother to hide his face from the peephole.

The door slowly opened. "Eldon?"

"Hello, Gavin."

"I'm in trouble, aren't I?"

The sentinels, who had been lined up along the wall out of sight, came up behind Eldon.

"I'm afraid so."

"You need to come with us," Vaughn said.

Gavin paused, but then in a flash, he tried to shut the door and run.

Eldon had anticipated this. He put his foot against the door to keep it open and grabbed his brother by the collar, much the way he used to when they were kids.

Gavin's body slammed against his own.

"It's over, little brother."

THIRTY-FIVE

WHEN SAXON and the others brought Gavin Conrad into the main house, Demi didn't know what she had been expecting, but this guy wasn't it. She couldn't believe this was the person who'd tried to kill her and Siya and abducted Kendall. He was practically a kid.

"You can take him downstairs. We can talk to him in the morning. I think everyone needs to get some rest right now. Some of you are going to have to relieve Chase, Ranulf, Zane, and Tegan tomorrow. I don't want anyone to be tired while they're out there," Vance said.

"You can't do this," Gavin said. "I was only following orders." He looked at his brother. "Eldon, why are you letting them do this to me?"

Eldon shook his head. "You did this to yourself, Gavin. The second you wouldn't let me take Kendall home. I tried to help you. I failed."

"Yeah, you did. Donny always said you were weak," Gavin shouted when he didn't get what he wanted from Eldon.

"Take him downstairs," Vance commanded.

Vaughn and Damien led Gavin around to the kitchen and then down the stairs to the basement.

Kendall got up from the couch where she'd been camped out since they brought her home. She made her way over to Eldon and put her hand on his arm while she spoke softly to him.

"What's down there?" Demi asked Saxon.

"A holding cell for prisoners."

"What's going to happen to him?"

Saxon shrugged. "That'll be up to Vance and Damien."

Vaughn and Damien came back upstairs and into the living room.

"Is he secure?" Vance asked.

They both nodded.

"Damien and I talked. Reid and Lachlan are on duty tonight. The rest of us, let's get to bed."

"We have a problem with that, boss," Saxon said.

Vance lifted his brow. "Oh?"

"Something has to be done about the bunkhouse. We just don't have enough room. With all the changes that have happened the last few years, we've been playing musical beds lately."

"So, what are you suggesting?"

"Unfortunately, nothing tonight, but I think you might consider expanding the bunkhouse."

"Yeah, Dad, it would be really nice if Sawyer and I didn't have to sleep on the couch when we were on duty," Vaughn said.

"You've been sleeping on the couch?"

"Yes. Where else would we sleep?"

"I just assumed you slept in your old room."

"Sawyer and I no longer have old rooms. Saxon and Camden share one, and Tegan and Reid share another. Then, one room is Kendall's, and the other is Ram's. Sometimes, one of us bunks with Ram, but if we're both on duty, one of us has the couch."

Vance ran his hand down his face. "This is a lot to take in right now after a long day." He sighed. "What do we do tonight?"

"I can sleep in my old room in the main house tonight," Vaughn said. "And Eldon can sleep in Payton's room."

"*I'll* be sleeping in Payton's room tonight, seeing as my mate is already upstairs in bed," Damien corrected.

"I can move back to my old bed," Camden said. "And Saxon can just deal with it."

"Where the hell have you been sleeping?" Vance asked.

"In Kendall's room. Saxon kicked me out."

Vance narrowed his eyes at Saxon.

"Because Demi's been staying with me," Saxon immediately protested. "We already have two to a room."

"They're sharing a bed," Camden said. "They just didn't want me around, so they could *do it*."

This time, Saxon narrowed his eyes at Camden and curled his lip in a threatening look.

"When I built that place, things were a lot easier," Vance said.

"Yeah, well, now, a lot of us have mates, and with the wolves and vampires trading with us, we need more room," Saxon said.

Demi didn't miss the fact that Saxon had said, "a lot of

us have mates," and wondered if he realized what he'd just spoken out loud.

"If only you knew someone with a construction business who could help," Vaughn said sarcastically.

"Very funny, son. I will take it into consideration," Vance said.

"That still leaves Eldon for tonight," Vaughn said.

"I can get a hotel room," Eldon said the same time Kendall said, "He can stay with me."

"Son, you are not getting a hotel room tonight. You're staying here, where you're safe. Plus, we have some more questions for you," Vance said.

"I don't really want to be alone," Kendall said to Eldon. "You can stay in the other bed."

Eldon nodded once. "Only if you're sure."

"I'm sure," she said.

Vance clapped his hands. "Let's go to bed then." He turned to go upstairs but stopped. "Oh, and, Reid?"

Reid, who'd been sitting in the corner, watching everyone else interact, stood. "Yes?"

"Find me everything you can about that property Kendall and Eldon were held at."

"I'll have it to you by morning."

"Lachlan?" Damien said.

"Yes?"

"I want the same thing."

Lachlan grinned at Reid. "Twenty bucks says I'll find all the information before you."

Reid grinned back. "You're on."

"Or you could just work together," Vance said as he went up the stairs.

"Competition is more fun," Reid said, but Demi doubted the alpha had even heard him.

"Let's go." Saxon grabbed Demi's hand, and they walked out of the main house, toward the bunkhouse. "I think you might want to call in to work tomorrow. It's going to be a big day. They need me here, and I worry about you at work."

"I already did," Demi told him.

"Thank God."

Demi laughed.

"I thought you'd argue with me."

She laughed again. "Not this time." She tilted her head. "Do you think it's safe for Siya to still be at work?"

"She's already there. Let her finish her shift. Now that you're here with me, I don't think anyone's going to target your friend. Besides, Ram won't let anything happen to her. You could always text her if you're worried."

"I already did," Demi said with a grin.

They headed to Saxon's room where Camden was already sitting on his bed in just a pair of shorts. Saxon growled.

"Get used to it," Camden said and slipped under the covers. He turned his back to them and put his pillow over his head.

"I don't think he's going anywhere," Demi said.

"Me eith—"

There was a knock at Saxon's open door, and the two of them turned.

"Hey, Saxon. Can I get some more clothes from you for Eldon to sleep in?"

"Oh, sure," Demi said. She went to Saxon's dresser and

grabbed a tee and shorts and brought them over to Kendall. "Here you go."

"Thank you," Kendall said and walked away.

"You're just going through my stuff like it's yours now, huh?"

"Were you going to say no?" Demi asked with a smile.

"No."

She lifted a shoulder. "Then, what's the problem?"

Saxon growled and hit the lights. He stood in front of Demi and kissed her as he guided her back to his bed. He pushed her down. "The problem is," he said in a hushed voice, "it's my stuff, and now, you owe me." His tone was playful, and she grinned.

"What do I owe you?" she asked.

"Get under the covers." He put his mouth next to her ear. "And take off all your clothes."

"But what about…"

Saxon knew what she meant. "He's sleeping. Just be really quiet."

"Me?"

"Take off your clothes, baby."

Demi did what Saxon had said but made sure the covers were pulled up to her chin.

He slipped in beside her after he took off his shirt and pants, so he was only in his boxers. He kissed her again and pulled the sheet over his head. He tongued each nipple, and Demi had to grab on to a pillow and cover her mouth with it.

Saxon kissed down her belly until he was between her legs. If getting head was a way of her owing him, she was going to do more things like giving away his clothes again.

Saxon bit down on the inside of her thigh as he pushed two fingers inside her.

She moaned against the pillow as quietly as she could.

Saxon knew how to make her squirm and keep her on edge, but tonight, he didn't do that. He put his mouth directly on her clit and sucked, and he used his fingers to rub her G-spot. Soon, she was rocking her hips over his hand, and before she knew it, her orgasm was upon her.

It had taken her an embarrassingly short amount of time to reach her climax, but she didn't care because it felt so good.

She kept the pillow over her face, but when she felt it was safe, she whipped it off her head to grab some air.

"Oh *my* God," came from the other bed, and Demi froze. "*That's it*. I'm sleeping on the couch."

She could feel Saxon moving against her leg, and she realized he was laughing.

Camden got up from his bed. "You two are disgusting," he said and stomped out of the room, practically slamming the door behind him.

Saxon flung the covers off his head.

"I thought you said he was sleeping?" Demi hissed at him.

Saxon crawled up her body. "I guess I was wrong. But the good news is, now, I can properly fuck you." Saxon pulled his boxers off his hard cock and pushed it inside her.

Demi clutched his back at the feel of him inside her. "More."

"Finally. Just the way it's supposed to be."

THIRTY-SIX

KENDALL SAT ON HER BED, waiting for Eldon to get done taking a shower. Despite being tired, she couldn't go to sleep until she made sure he was settled.

If only she had her phone to keep her busy, but that was probably long gone. If Reid hadn't been able to track her from day one, she was sure the members of the Pure Pride whatever had gotten rid of it.

"Hey."

Kendall jumped from her bed at Eldon's greeting. Her hand automatically went to her small bump, and she forced her arm to drop. "Are you okay?"

"Yeah." He cautiously stepped into the room. "Are you sure it's okay I stay here?"

"Yes. I changed the sheets on the other bed while you were showering, so they're fresh for you."

Eldon stepped forward. "That's not what I meant." He looked around. "I mean…" He sighed. "Is it weird that I'm staying here after everything that happened to us? It almost seems surreal now."

"It does, kind of." She held out her arm. "But please, we both need to sleep. We've been sleeping in the same room for a few days now."

"That's because we had to."

"Are you saying you don't want to be here?" she asked.

"No." Eldon shook his head. "No. I don't know what I'm saying. I just feel…" He smiled. "Never mind. Let's go to bed." He walked over to the spare bed in her room and slid under the covers.

Kendall turned off the light and got in her own bed. She closed her eyes, but sleep did not come. She could hear Eldon fidgeting over on his bed, too.

"Can't sleep?" she asked.

"No. I thought I would be out so fast."

"Same here."

"I think I'm just worried about my brother."

"What he did to us was wrong."

"I know. And I think he deserves to be punished. But I'm worried that Vance will order his death."

Kendall rolled on her side. "What do you think should happen to him?"

"I honestly don't know. As a detective, part of me thinks that I should turn him over to the police and have him sent to prison. He fired shots in a residential area and planted a car bomb. The public needs to know that it's unacceptable and that people can't get away with that."

Kendall grimaced. "A shifter stuck in a tiny cell. That sounds awful."

"Then, maybe he shouldn't have broken the law."

"Have you told Vance and Damien how you feel?"

"Do I even have that right? Vance's and Damien's words are law."

"You were your brother's victim. And Vance would never punish you for sharing your thoughts. Maybe prison is the right answer for your brother. He might go away for a long time."

"Not only would it show humans that they can't get away with those actions, but it would also show other shifters. Shifters who belong to the wrong kind of groups."

"I think that's an excellent point. You should definitely talk to Vance and Damien."

"I think I will."

"What do you think they should do about Donald Wright?"

"That's not up to me," Eldon said.

"Answer it anyway."

"I think shifter law is appropriate for him."

In other words, Eldon was okay with his death. It would make the world safer if he was gone.

"But, at least, I got to meet you."

"What?" Kendall asked.

"I'm glad I met you."

"Really?" She laughed. "I'm pretty sure I made your life miserable."

"Nah. Besides, the way it ended was pretty dang good."

Kendall closed her eyes and remembered the way he'd pushed her into the wall as he pushed inside her.

Eldon groaned. "I thought your heat was over."

Her eyes flew open. "It is." She chuckled uncomfortably. "I was just remembering."

"Thank God."

"Thank God what?"

"Thank God I'm not the only one," Eldon said.

"You've been thinking about it, too?"

Eldon laughed as if she'd truly said something funny. "Kendall, I will never forget the way it felt to be inside you. Even though we were hungry and wet and scraped up, it was the best sex I'd ever had in my life."

Kendall liked knowing he felt that way. "What if it's just the hormones and the pheromones talking?"

"I suppose you could be right. I've never been with a woman during her heat before, so I don't know the answer to that. But I suspect sex with you would be good anyway." Eldon groaned. "I hope that didn't sound creepy."

Kendall chuckled.

"I think it's just weird that we avoided even touching each other for so long, and then we had crazy sex outside an abandoned gas station. And now…now, I don't know where we stand. Are we friends? Survivors? More?" Eldon asked.

"Is that why you asked if it was okay if you slept in here?"

"Yes. I didn't want anything to be awkward between us. Too late, huh?"

"Do you think we'll ever fall asleep?"

"Oh," Eldon replied at her change of subject. "I suppose. Eventually."

Kendall pushed the covers off her body. "I don't want to do eventually." She walked over to Eldon's bed, pulled her pajama shirt off, and pushed her shorts and underwear to her feet. She took his hand and lifted it to her neck, carried it across her chest, down her stomach, and in between her legs where she was already starting to get wet.

Eldon hissed. "You are so beautiful," he said and pushed a finger into her. "Still hot and tight. Maybe it wasn't just your heat."

Kendall threw back the comforter and pulled Eldon's shorts off. He took his hand from between her legs long enough to pull his shirt over his head. He put his hand back and pushed two fingers into her.

She grabbed on to his arm to steady herself.

"You okay?" he asked.

"More than." Kendall wrapped her fingers around Eldon's hardness.

"Damn," he said breathlessly.

Kendall pulled his hand from between her thighs and got up on the bed and straddled him. "Are *you* okay with this?" she asked.

"If you don't put me inside you, I just might die."

Kendall laughed and slowly sank down on Eldon's cock. "Oh my God," she said with a gasp.

"What?"

Kendall leaned over and kissed his chest as she began to rock her hips. "I didn't think you'd still feel this good."

Eldon cupped her ass and raised his hips. "I'll take that as a compliment."

She kissed her way up his neck to his ear. "You should." She increased the pace of her movements. "Is it crazy that we're doing this?"

"Fuck no. It'd only be crazy if we stopped." He kissed her mouth. "For the record, please don't stop."

"Are you going to come?"

"Yes."

"Good. I want to feel it," she told him. For some reason, she needed to feel it.

Eldon gripped her hips and yanked her down to him as he cried out. Kendall felt his seed fill her once more, and she began to climax around him. She hadn't expected it to feel so good now that her heat was over.

She rotated her hips over him to keep her orgasm going for as long as she could, her body more in control than her mind, almost as much as the last time they'd had sex.

Eldon was still shuddering underneath her, and Kendall lifted her hips, withdrawing him completely from her body. The barbs on his cock sent tiny little signals through her womb, and she came again.

"Fuck," Eldon exclaimed as she sank down on him again, the barbs causing another orgasm, this time for both of them.

Kendall crumpled on top of Eldon as she felt him throb and empty inside her.

He rubbed her back. "Holy shit."

"Yeah," she said, smiling against his neck.

"What was with you pulling me out and pushing me back in after I came?"

"I don't know. I just did it."

"Well, it felt amazing."

"Good to know." Kendall slid off Eldon's body to his side, and her eyes drifted shut. "I don't think I can move."

He turned onto his side, put an arm around her, and kissed her head. "That's all right with me. You can stay right here."

Kendall pushed her nose to his skin and did just that.

THIRTY-SEVEN

"HEY, SIYA?"

Siya looked up from the med cart to see her coworker, Joanne, walking up to her. "Yeah?"

"There is a man at the nurses' station who wants to speak to you."

"Oh?"

"Yeah, he's very tall and very muscular. And handsome as hell." Joanne fanned her face like she was hot.

"Oh, that's just Ram."

"Honey, that man isn't *just* anything." Joanne gave Siya a pointed look.

Joanne had a point.

"Let me finish getting this, and I'll go see what he wants."

Joanne shut the med drawer.

"What did you do that for?"

"I'll help you with your patient. You go see what he wants. Don't keep him waiting."

"Okay."

Siya headed to the nurses' station, and when she rounded the corner, it was indeed Ram waiting there. He was talking to the health unit coordinator and another nurse, but when he saw her coming, his face broke into a grin.

She liked the way that made her feel.

"Hey, what's up?" she asked.

So far, Ram had kept a safe distance from her. He'd drop her off at night, and in the morning, someone else would pick her up.

"Is there any way you can get off work a little early tonight?"

She looked down at her watch. She still had two hours to go. "Not really. We're almost at capacity. I can't just leave my patients for someone else to cover. What's going on?"

Ram narrowed his eyes. "Didn't Demi text you and explain?"

Siya shrugged. "I don't know. Maybe. It's been so busy; I've hardly had time to eat, much less check my phone."

Ram frowned. "They're overworking you."

"I just told you, we're almost full. Anyway, why do you want me to get off work early?"

"Kendall is back, and they also brought in the guy who is responsible for shooting at you and blowing up your car."

"You're shitting me?"

Ram smiled. "Dead serious."

"Why do you need me to leave early though?"

"Everyone is busy, and I'd like to take you home before the sun comes up. I don't want to leave you on your own."

"Okay, um…" Siya's thoughts were everywhere. "Let me

think. The nursing supervisor comes on in half an hour. I will ask if I can leave when she gets here."

"Great. I'll swing back around."

Siya said good-bye and turned around. There were several pairs of eyes on her. "Nothing to see here."

"I was hoping he'd pull you into his arms and kiss you," Joanne said.

Siya laughed. "This is not television. This is real life. And no man is touching me until I get out of my scrubs and have taken a shower."

"Oh, yeah, this is true. Too many germs," Joanne agreed.

"See," Siya said and went to wrap things up with each of her patients.

If she didn't leave any work to be done unless the patient hit the nurse button, then hopefully, taking off an hour and a half early wouldn't be a problem.

She threw herself into her work. She didn't bother to see who was on as nursing supervisor that day, and she lost track of time. Ram came back around, and she held up her finger to tell him one moment. Then, she went to talk to the nurse in charge.

She knocked on the door of the office, and when the door swung open, her hopes dropped. It was Lou. Lou hated her. To be fair, Lou hated everybody, and the only way he'd okay someone going home early was if they had a limb falling off.

"Can I help you with something, Siya?"

She hated even asking this jackass anything, but she didn't have a choice. "Would it be okay if I left early?"

"Why?" Lou's eyebrow rose in a look that said, *You'd better make this good*. "Are you ill?"

"No."

"Is it an emergency?"

"Not per se. But it is important."

"Hmm," Lou said and tapped his chin. As if he were actually thinking about it. "We're full of patients, and didn't Lindsey call in sick last night?"

Shit. "Yes."

"Then, no. Sorry." Lou took a step back and shut the door.

"Dick," Siya said under her breath. She reluctantly turned around and headed back to the nurses' station. She shook her head as she approached Ram. "My boss said no. I'm sorry."

"It's fine. You tried."

"I'll just grab an Uber when I get off work."

"No, Siya, I'll wait."

She shook her head again. "No, I don't want you to get sick or whatever it is. I'll be fine."

Lou came around the corner. He'd probably give her extra work if he caught her talking.

"Look, I have to run. I'll see you when I get back to the bunkhouse." She turned and walked away. "Bye," she said over her shoulder and quickly moved down the hall and out of Lou's view.

The last thing she saw was Ram pulling his phone from his pocket, hitting a few buttons, and putting it to his ear.

☾

Lou handed out extra assignments anyway. By the time Siya went to the locker room, it was half an hour after her shift. Thank heavens she'd told Ram to go on without her.

Siya quickly grabbed her food from the fridge and her purse from the locker room. Thankfully, she was done for the weekend, but she wanted to get out of there.

She pulled her phone from her bag as she made her way to the front door. She pulled up her Uber app, put in her info, and went to check her texts to kill some time.

There was the one from Demi telling her about Kendall being back. It was such a relief. And there was also a text from Ram.

Ram: Call me when you're done. I'll be waiting for you.

Siya quickly dialed him.

"Hello?"

"I told you not to wait for me."

"Are you done?"

"Yes. Where are you?"

"Headed your way."

Siya turned and saw Ram striding down the hall. Damn, he looked good even if she was supposed to be mad at him for waiting.

She quickly canceled her Uber and looked up at Ram when he reached her. "You're crazy, you know that?"

He put his arm around her. "Nah. I just don't want anything happening to you."

"What about the sun?"

"I got it taken care of." He squeezed her shoulder. "Let's go."

THIRTY-EIGHT

ELDON SAT in a room with his cat-shifter alpha and the wolf-shifter alpha and explained why he should be allowed to take his brother into the police. He'd thought about it all night, and he knew he had to try to plead for Gavin's life.

"I don't know if I can do that, son," Vance said.

"I think the asshole deserves everything that's coming to him," Damien said. "He kidnapped one of my sentinels."

"With all due respect, he kidnapped me, too," Eldon said. "And, if I bring him in, that's one of the things I'm going to charge him with."

Damien crossed his arms across his chest. "How exactly do you see this going down?"

"I'm going to tell my captain that I discovered my brother was behind the shooting and the bombing, and when I found out, he locked me up in a room."

Vance rubbed his chin, deep in thought. "And what are you going to tell them when they asked where your brother kept you?"

"The truth," Eldon said. "Reid and Lachlan said that

the building is owned by some holding company. It's a piece of shit. I'll let them think it was abandoned."

"If it was abandoned, then how did you end up there?"

"Gavin found it when he needed a place to hide his crimes."

"It could work," Vance said.

"Okay then, why did your brother commit the crime?" Damien asked challengingly. He obviously didn't agree with Vance.

Eldon shrugged. "I'm sure the DA and prosecution will come up with something. That's not my job as a detective. I'm just supposed to bring him to justice and make sure he'll be punished."

"Oh, he'll be punished all right," Damien said. "There's no need to send him to jail."

"Oh, and who will know about it? Will everyone in the metro area know? The state of Minnesota? The country?" Eldon shook his head. "I bet not even all the shifters will know."

Damien opened his mouth but quickly slammed it shut.

Vance turned to the wolf. "He has a good point. If Gavin Conrad is punished in a court of law, we can spread the word to shifters everywhere about why he's being punished. Humans will think one thing, but we'll know another."

"I still think he deserves to die."

Eldon winced.

"Perhaps that punishment would be too easy for him, Damien. This is a young man who needs to suffer for what he's done."

"I don't like it. He kidnapped Kendall, Vance."

"I know. He also kidnapped one of my shifters and tried to kill another. Simply because she was born half-human."

Damien ran his hands through his hair. "You're right. And I hate that you're right."

Vance looked at Eldon. "I will agree to it on two conditions."

"What are the conditions?" Eldon asked.

"One, you make sure that Demi is okay with this. And Kendall and Siya, too. They might not have been his targets, but they were caught in the cross fire. No pun intended."

"Done. And what's the other condition?" Eldon asked.

"You find out where Donald Wright is."

"But I have no idea. I've never hung out with him outside the clubhouse. We're not friends."

Vance put his hands on his hips. "I know. But I bet your brother has an idea of where he is hiding. And, if he doesn't, he'll know how to find out." Vance looked at his watch. "No one has shown up at the clubhouse yet to bring you food. Your brother can call and tell him there's trouble."

Eldon swallowed. He wanted this to work. He didn't want his brother to die. But he didn't know if Gavin would go along with it. He took a deep breath. "I agree." He just hoped Gavin would, too. Eldon looked at Damien. "And what about you? What are your terms?"

"The same."

Eldon's eyebrows flew up. "Really?"

Damien nodded. "That, and he has to apologize to Kendall, Demi, and Siya."

Jeez. And Eldon had thought the last demand was hard. "Deal."

243

"All right then. You go and speak with your brother. We'll go break the news to everyone else."

"Okay."

"Once you get down there, send Vaughn and Raven up here," Vance said.

"Will do."

Eldon slowly made his way down the stairs to where his brother was being held. He met Vaughn and Raven at the bottom. "You two are supposed to head upstairs. I need to talk to my brother."

"Are you going to tell him his fate?" Vaughn asked.

"Yeah. Something like that."

Vaughn clapped Eldon on the back. "Good luck, man."

Raven and Vaughn went up the stairs, and Eldon entered the room his brother was in.

Gavin turned and sneered when he saw Eldon. "Have you come to tell me how fucked I am? Or did they send you to kill me yourself?"

"Your mind has been poisoned way too long, Gavin."

"Whatever."

"I've actually come to offer you life."

Gavin's eyes lit up. "No shit? What are you going to do? Break me out of here?"

"No, Gavin, it's not that simple." Eldon explained the things that would be required of him and how he would probably go to prison for the rest of his life.

"I'll go crazy in there," Gavin said.

"But you'd be alive."

Gavin wildly shook his head back and forth. "I'd rather die."

Eldon's shoulders slumped. "Okay. It's your decision."

He turned to go back upstairs. It looked like Vance and Damien should have waited to break the news.

"Eldon?" Gavin said softly.

Eldon stopped. "Yeah?"

"If I do this, would you come and visit me?"

"Of course."

Eldon heard Gavin take in a deep breath.

"Tell them I'll do it."

SAXON STOOD, arms folded, as Gavin Conrad was brought upstairs in cuffs and silver bracelets to keep him from shifting. He still couldn't believe they were working with the asshole. Yes, they needed to find Donald Wright, but this man had almost killed his Demi. And, for that, he deserved to die.

Others were giving Gavin dirty looks across the room, so at least Saxon knew he wasn't the only one unhappy with this plan.

The one thing stopping him from taking justice into his own hands was the fact that Eldon had rescued Kendall. Eldon had requested his brother not be killed. Saxon hoped that Eldon knew that they no longer owed Eldon anything, and their debt was clear.

Vance clapped his hands together. "Okay, crew, I know that many of you are not happy with the deal Damien and I made with Eldon, but you don't have to be. You just have to follow orders and do what we tell you to do. Understand?"

Everyone nodded their heads. Even Saxon.

Vance looked at Gavin. "Has your brother explained everything to you? Do you understand that you must do what we say, or the deal is off?"

Gavin nodded and hung his head.

Vance sighed. "I guess it's time to bring Demi, Kendall, and Siya in here."

Damien opened the front door of the house. "Thanks for waiting, ladies. Come on in."

The three of them entered the room, and Saxon immediately went over to them.

"Are you okay? I know it's not easy, seeing him here." He pointed to Gavin.

Siya was scared—Saxon could smell it—but she had her game face on. Demi, on the other hand, looked like she wanted to kill the guy. Saxon had to hide his grin; he was so proud.

"Let's just get this over with," Demi said, "so he can get what he deserves."

Saxon nodded and led them over to the couch.

"Please sit," Vance said.

The females sat, and Vance began to lay out the plan that Eldon had come up with. When he was done, the three women sat there, not saying much.

Kendall spoke first, "Eldon told me his thoughts last night, and I support it. Personally, I think his brother will go a little crazy in prison, not being able to shift and run free."

There were murmurs across the room.

"You bring up a good point, Kendall," Damien said.

Saxon had to agree. Maybe prison wouldn't be such a sweet deal after all.

Siya raised her arm. "I'm okay with it. As a human, I

grew up with the human justice system. While I don't want to judge you on yours, sir, killing him outright does make me uncomfortable."

Vance nodded. "Demi?"

"As long as I know he'll never hurt anyone again, I'm okay with it, too." She looked at Eldon. "You promise not to plead his case and talk the judge down for a lighter sentence?"

"Yes, ma'am," Eldon said.

"Fine. Let's do this then."

"Sorry, babe, but you're not doing anything," Saxon said. Before she could protest, he said, "You need to let the professionals handle this. This is our job."

"Fine," she said again. "Can I at least stay and listen?"

Saxon looked at Vance, who nodded.

Siya stood. "Thanks for everything, but I'm going to bed."

Demi stood as well.

"Keep me updated," Siya told Demi.

Siya left, and Demi sat back down.

"Kendall, you're more than welcome to stay, but I'm going to ask you to sit this one out," Damien said. "You just came off your heat, and most of us feel like you already did your part."

Kendall put her hand up. "I'm going to stop you there. I am okay with it. I am still recovering, and I'm not going to put others in danger for a little revenge."

Damien looked relieved.

Kendall laughed. "You need to have more faith in me."

"About a half hour ago, Zane called us and said that someone had shown up at the clubhouse with breakfast.

Raven and Zane are on their way here with him now. He says his name is Roy. Do you know who that is?" Vance asked Eldon.

"Yes."

Vance turned to Gavin. "Young man, I need you to listen now. I want you to call Donny and tell him that Roy called you to go to the clubhouse this morning because he couldn't make it. And then you're going to tell him Kendall's heat is over and that the exchange can happen today. Do you understand?"

Gavin nodded.

"I need to hear you say it."

"Yes, sir."

"If you try to send him some kind of message to not show, we'll know. And you'll live to regret it," Damien said.

"I understand," Gavin said.

☾

Eldon stood with Gavin in the clubhouse, waiting for Donny to show up. So far, their plan was going well. Gavin had made the call to Donny, and when Donny had called Vance five minutes later, they knew he'd believed what Gavin told him. But Eldon had no idea what would happen when Donny actually showed.

The sound of a car coming up the drive made Eldon's heart beat faster. He went to the window and peeked out. It was Donny's car.

Eldon scanned the area. Everyone was safely hidden from Donny's view. He just hoped the wind didn't change direction in the next few minutes.

He turned to Gavin. "I know you're nervous, but you need to calm down a little. I can smell your fear."

"What about you?" his brother snapped.

"I'm trying my best to remain calm, too. But I've also had years of practice doing it because of my job. I'll be good to go once Donny's here."

The car came to a stop, and the engine was cut.

"Showtime, little brother." Eldon pulled a pair of cutters from his back pocket and cut Gavin's zip ties. "Go to the door. Greet him. And make sure you say his name, so the others know who he is."

Gavin nodded and went to the door. Eldon hid behind it as it was opened. Since Eldon had been at the clubhouse for a week, his scent was already expected to be there.

"Gavin," Donny said after getting out of his car. "Are you as excited about today as I am?"

"Uh…yes?" Gavin said.

Fuck, Gavin, pull it together. Sound more confident.

Donny laughed. "You should sound happier. You're the one who brought this whole thing together."

Shit. Don't feel guilty, Gavin. And don't do anything stupid.

"I-I guess," Gavin stammered.

Donny's footsteps stopped. "Gavin?"

"Yes."

"Do I have anything to be worried about when I walk into the clubhouse?"

Gavin hesitated for only a moment. "No." But it was enough.

"You fucking lying sack of shit."

Eldon came out from behind the door. "It's over, Donny. It's time to surrender."

Donny turned and ran for his vehicle as the sentinels appeared. He stopped short when he saw he was surrounded by big cats and wolves. He must have realized he'd never make it to his car fast enough.

Donny shifted into his cat and took off running in the opposite direction.

The cat-shifter closest to him, with a brown-and-blond coat, went after him. Eldon had a feeling Saxon wasn't going to let Donny get far.

Eldon grabbed his brother by the collar of his shirt when he went to run after them. "I can't let you go after him." He spun Gavin around and put a new set of cuffs on him.

"I'm not going after him," Gavin said.

Eldon raised his brow.

"I swear. I just want to see what's going to happen."

"Suit yourself." Eldon had a good feeling about what he was about to see. He took his brother by the cuffs and led him outside.

Not far from the building, a naked Saxon stood, covered in blood, staring at the ground. The other sentinels approached and shifted into their human forms, too, but Saxon was the only one dirty.

On the ground at Saxon's feet lay Donny, dead with his throat ripped out.

Gavin turned away when they reached the body.

"Just be thankful that's not you," Eldon told his brother. "Because it could have been."

FORTY

SIYA WAS BEING PULLED from a deep sleep from someone shaking her awake.

"Siya, Siya, Siya."

"What is it, Demi?"

She knew her friend would only wake her if it was something important. She sat up in bed as Ram did the same thing from his.

"Donald Wright is dead."

"Really?"

"Yes. He's really dead. And Gavin's headed to the police station as we speak."

"Wow." Siya looked at Ram. "That's great news."

He smiled, and she realized she was going home very soon.

"It is," Demi said, grinning. "We're finally safe."

"What about all the other members?"

"Eldon's already on it. He knows all their names, and he's going to get a list of addresses. They'll be picked up soon."

"What will happen to them?"

Demi shrugged. "No idea. But I'm not going to worry about it now. I'm in too good of a mood." She jumped off of Siya's bed. "Well, I'll let you get back to sleep. I'll talk to you soon."

Demi shut the door, and Siya said, "I don't think that's going to happen."

"What's not going to happen?" Ram asked.

"Sleeping? After news like that, my heart is racing."

He smiled and got up from his bed. "It is good news." He walked over to Siya and sat down next to her. "I suppose you'll be going home now."

"I guess so," she said, looking into Ram's eyes. They were yellow and filled with heat.

Siya pushed the covers off her legs and got up on her knees.

"What are you doing?" he asked.

She put her arms around his neck. "This," she said as she leaned down and kissed him.

Ram pulled her to his body and kissed her back.

Siya groaned. He tasted good and knew how to work his mouth. She slipped her tongue inside and scraped it over his sharp tooth. Rather than being scared, it only made her hot. She moved to sit on Ram's lap when he pulled away.

"What's wrong?" she asked.

"We can't do this." Ram was breathing hard, and she could see the erection in his underwear.

She ran her hand down his hair. "Yes, we can," she assured him.

If he was worried about her, he had no reason to be.

Ram gently set her on the bed and stood. "No, we can't.

I'm sorry." He turned, picked up his jeans, and left the room.

Siya sat there, alone and confused. She had been sure that he liked her, but it seemed she'd been wrong.

Thank God she was leaving soon because she felt like a fool. And, if she never saw Ram again, she'd die quite happy.

She slid off the bed and began packing.

☽

Demi paced back and forth between the living room and the kitchen of the bunkhouse, waiting for Saxon to return. When he came through the door, the two of them stood there for a moment, just watching each other.

"You're bloody," Demi said.

His clothes were clean, but she could still clearly see his messy body.

"I am," Saxon said, standing tall and proud.

Demi stepped forward and grabbed Saxon's hand. She laced his fingers with her own and led him down the hall into the bathroom.

She flipped on the water and turned around to Saxon. She slowly lifted his shirt from his body.

"I'm not hurt," he told her.

She slipped her fingers under the waistband of his shorts and met his eyes. They were still in his cat form. "Were you the one who killed him?"

"Donald?"

"Yes."

"I was."

"That's the hottest thing a guy has ever done for me."

Saxon hauled her into his arms and kissed her. She didn't even care that he was covered in blood and most likely getting it on her clothes.

"Take a shower with me. I want to fuck you against the wall."

Demi kissed him again. "You had me at 'take a shower.'"

☾

Several hours later, Ram headed over to the main house for the meeting Vance had called. It had rained again, so the air was damp. The starless sky and gloomy weather seemed to fit his mood despite the good news they'd all received earlier.

The room was mostly full by the time he got there, and he made his way toward the back.

Even though he was trying to blend in, he could feel eyes on him. When he turned, he saw that Siya was watching him.

She quickly looked away.

He felt awful about turning her down earlier, but he'd had to.

He was way too hungry to be messing around with a human.

He thought he'd be okay, but when her tongue had scraped his fang, his hunger had flared. He'd been outside in the sun twice that week, and he needed to feed. He couldn't drink Siya's blood though. It wouldn't be enough to sustain him, and humans couldn't lose as much as vampires and shifters.

Besides, he knew she had kissed him because she was going home soon, and she had seen it as her last chance. It didn't sit well with him. He didn't know why because, if it had been anyone else, he'd have been cool with it. With Siya, it rubbed him the wrong way.

"Good evening, everyone," Vance said from the middle of the room with Damien and Eldon beside him. "Donald Wright is dead, Eldon here has turned his brother over to police custody, and we are rounding up other members of the Pure Pride Power."

"What's going to happen to them?" Saxon asked.

"It depends on their involvement and what they knew about Gavin Conrad's plan. We'll find a fitting punishment for all along with teaching and showing them that all species are welcome."

"What about the clubhouse?" Vaughn asked.

"Eldon gave the location to the police. We scrubbed Donald's blood from the grass, and thanks to the rain, we're safe. Both Eldon and I have connections within the crime lab unit. They will eliminate any trace of Kendall they find. DNA, saliva, hair, et cetera." Vance looked at Kendall. "We're doing our best to keep you out of this."

It had already been discussed that, if the police found out Kendall had been kidnapped, it would lead to too many questions and only cause more lies to cover things up. Humans couldn't find out about shifters, and they wouldn't understand Kendall watching over Demi. That would only lead to more questions of why, and the police certainly couldn't find out that Demi had killed a human in self-defense.

This was maybe why they should have left justice in the hands of the shifters, but no one had asked his opinion.

Ram's phone vibrated, and he saw that his friend Bianca was outside. He quietly left the room and headed out.

"Hey," he called out.

"Hey yourself," the dark-haired female called back. "You doing okay?"

"Yeah, yeah. I just need to feed. Let's go over to the bunkhouse to my room."

Bianca smiled. "Lead the way."

☾

Siya watched Ram leave the room and knew her time here was over. She raised her hand.

"Yes, Siya?" Vance said.

"Does this mean Demi and I can go home? Are we safe now?"

Vance looked at Damien and Eldon and then to Saxon. "I think you are. But you know that, if you need anything, you can call."

Siya jumped up from the couch and smiled. While things hadn't worked out with Ram, she was grateful for everything Vance and the sentinels had done. She put her hand out to him. "Thank you."

Vance smiled and shook her hand. "You're very welcome."

"Do you need help with your stuff?" Demi asked.

Siya turned around to her friend. "Nope. I already have my car packed."

"Wow. That was fast."

That's because I want to get out of here. "I'm efficient."

Demi hugged Siya. "Call me when you get home."

"I will."

The two of them separated, and Siya walked outside. When she reached her car, she looked at the bunkhouse one last time.

Ram's light was on, and in that moment, she decided to say good-bye to him. She was a grown woman, and while she'd been humiliated earlier, she didn't want Ram to know that he'd affected her that much. He'd done a lot to protect her after all, and he deserved a thank-you.

She quietly let herself in the bunkhouse and listened for any sounds. The house was still.

The light from Ram's room flooded the dark hall, but when she rounded the corner of the bedroom, she was unprepared for what she saw.

A beautiful woman was sitting on Ram's lap. Her eyes were closed. His mouth was on one side of her neck while his hand was on the other side, holding her close as if he was afraid she'd leave.

The scene was very intimate, and Siya felt her stomach drop.

She must have made a noise because the lady opened her eyes.

"Ram," she said, shaking his arm.

Ram pulled his mouth away and licked the female's throat from where he'd clearly been feeding. He turned his gaze toward the open door. "Siya," he said.

He didn't even attempt to move the woman from his lap.

"I-I just came to say good-bye and thank you. Thank

you," she managed to say before she turned and bolted. Heat flooded her cheeks, and she felt sick.

No wonder he hadn't wanted her kissing him. He had a beautiful vampire in his life.

"Siya," Ram called out, but she ignored him.

She ran for her car, turned the engine over, and sped off. She'd already told herself she never wanted to see Ram again, but this time, she really and truly meant it.

FORTY-ONE

THE MEETING BROKE UP, and Kendall approached Eldon. They had a weird dynamic going on. Part of him was still a stranger, yet he'd been inside her.

This was probably why she didn't do one-night stands. They weren't her thing.

"How's your brother?"

Eldon nodded. "Good. Considering."

"And you? You didn't show up for a week, and then you told your boss you'd been kidnapped by your own brother. They must have thought you were crazy for a moment."

Eldon chuckled. "I'd go more with stunned."

"Well, I hope everything works out."

"It will." Eldon crossed his arms across his chest. "You know, I'm going to be under a lot of scrutiny. In case it somehow gets leaked that there was an unknown female in that office, it's probably best that we…"

"Don't see each other," Kendall finished for him. "I agree."

"You do?"

"Yes. I don't want to be involved with the case. I don't want them to know I was there. I don't want to have to lie about what my job is or why I was at the bombing. I'm tired. I just want my life to go back to normal."

Eldon dropped his arms, and it looked like he was going to reach for her hand, but he stopped. "You know, things are going to be different now. No matter what."

Kendall smiled. "I know, Eldon. This isn't my first rodeo. I'm not going to hide away. I will talk to someone about what I've been through. I'm not going to pretend it didn't happen. But I also don't want to pretend that I was just some person who happened to see what was happening when Demi and Siya were getting shot." She pushed her fingers into her chest. "What I do is important. I trained hard to be a sentinel. And I don't want to diminish my role because humans can't find out about us."

"Wow," was all Eldon said.

"Wow what?"

"You are crazy strong. I understand how you feel. I think it's why I became a police officer and then detective. I can put my heightened skills to good use." He smiled off into the distance. "I love it when I figure something out and shock my partner." He looked back at Kendall. "I might not get credit for being a shifter, but I get credit for my skills."

She smiled. She liked that he understood her. She held her hand out to him. "Despite the circumstances, I'm glad I met you."

Eldon shook her hand and pulled her into a hug. "Me, too."

Kendall pulled away. "You stay safe, okay?"

Eldon lost his smile. "You, too."

"I will. Good luck with everything."

"Thanks."

"Bye, Eldon."

"Later, Kendall."

☽

Saxon walked in silence on the way back to the bunkhouse after the meeting. It had been an eventful day, and he didn't feel like making small talk.

When they reached his room, Demi pulled out her bag and set it on his bed.

"What are you doing?"

She picked up a shirt of hers she'd found on the floor. "Packing. Vance gave me the all-clear to go home."

Saxon moved her knapsack out of the way and sat in front of her. "You don't have to go tonight." He didn't want her to go tonight.

Demi bit her bottom lip. "Are you sure?"

He picked up her hand. "Do you want to leave right now?"

"Not really?"

Saxon smiled. "Is that a statement or a question?"

She pushed her blonde hair behind her ear. "I wouldn't mind staying with you one more night."

He grinned and cupped her hips, pulling her to him. "Great. Let's have a naked sleepover."

Demi ran her hands through his hair. "All our sleepovers are naked sleepovers."

"We'd better not break tradition then."

The two of them undressed each other and got under

Saxon's sheets. He put his arm around Demi, pulled her back to his front, and relaxed.

"What? No sex tonight?"

Saxon shrugged even though she couldn't see him. "I just feel like holding you."

Demi brushed her fingers up and down his arm that was around her. "I suppose we did have some amazing sex in the shower earlier."

Saxon closed his eyes at the memory of her kissing him while he was covered in Donald Wright's blood. Demi didn't care that he'd killed a man. And, when he'd pushed her against the wall as he pushed inside her body, she'd cried out and clung to him.

"You okay back there?" Demi asked, interrupting his hot memory.

He cleared his throat. "Of course. Why wouldn't I be?"

"You made a weird noise. And your hard-on is poking me in the ass."

Saxon laughed and kissed her shoulder. "Sorry about that. I was thinking about our time in the shower."

"That would explain the erection."

"Hey, you brought it up."

She laughed. "Are you sure you don't want to do it?" She turned her head and looked at him. "This is the last time you're going to have a live-in booty call."

Saxon got up on his elbow and looked down at her with a frown. "Hey. You are not just some booty call."

Demi turned and faced him.

He rolled her onto her back. "Hey. You're not," he said, looking her in the eyes.

She smiled, but she almost looked…sad. "Come here."

Saxon lifted an eyebrow, and Demi grabbed his head and brought it down to her mouth.

Okay, so she didn't want to talk. He would show her how he felt.

Demi tried to rush him, but he wouldn't have it. She grabbed his cock, and he pulled her hand away. She dug her nails into his back, and he pushed her hands over her head.

He was going to make her remember their last night together.

((

Saxon made love to Demi's whole body. He kissed, licked, and sucked each breast. He did the same to her neck and her stomach. And, when she thought she just might go insane, he *slowly* pushed into her pussy.

She wanted to get back at him for torturing her, but her body betrayed her, and she came right away. This time, when she clawed at his back, it wasn't to rev him up; it was to keep him inside her as long as possible.

Saxon continued to thrust, and her orgasm just kept going and going. It was as if someone had put a battery inside her.

He pushed her hair out of her face and fisted the back of it. "That's it, baby." Thrust. Thrust. "Keep coming for me."

She gasped, and Saxon guided her mouth to his shoulder.

He nipped her neck. "I want you to bite me. Make me come as hard as you are right now."

Demi bit down on Saxon, wanting to mark him with her

bite. It wouldn't last forever, but for this brief moment in time, it would show that Saxon was hers.

Her orgasm started to recede, and she noticed her jaw ached from the force of her bite, so she carefully let go.

Saxon kissed her as he still made love to her. He lifted his head and looked down at her. "That was amazing." He smiled. "And, now, it's my turn."

He tilted her head to the side, but he didn't really need to, as she was already baring her neck to him.

Saxon bit down as his body shuddered and shook. She felt his barbs swell inside her, and she knew she'd never forget this moment.

After their incredible sex session, Saxon lay behind her again, cuddling her close to him, and fell asleep.

Demi gave herself a half hour to enjoy their last night together before she cautiously untangled herself from his arms. She turned around and watched Saxon sleep as she felt her eyes well with tears.

Being here with him, the sentinels, and her alpha had almost been like a dream come true. She felt like she could truly be herself, and she would only admit to it at this moment that she'd fallen in love with Saxon.

And that was why she needed to leave. He was a lifelong bachelor, and she'd done the unthinkable. Never fall for the permanently single guy.

But maybe that was Demi's MO. She'd had a dad who died, a mother who'd left her to be raised by someone else, and a grandmother who could never really love her and who had ended up dying on her, too.

The people in her life always left her, and if she turned

the tables and left now, she wouldn't have to worry about Saxon telling her good-bye.

This time, she would be in control.

She quietly packed her bag and stopped at the hall. She looked into his room one last time.

"Good-bye," she whispered.

And then she was out the door.

FORTY-TWO

ONE WEEK LATER

DEMI ROLLED onto her stomach and grabbed her phone. It was Saturday morning, and she should be sleeping in, but she'd just spent the last twenty minutes or so staring at her popcorn ceiling.

She scanned a little social media but ultimately ended up at her messages. Her thumb hovered over Saxon's name before she finally hit it.

She hadn't heard from him since she moved back to her house, and every day, she was disappointed. It only showed her that she'd been right in leaving because he hadn't even attempted to get her back. It was good that her logical brain had seen this coming. Unfortunately, her stupid heart had held out hope.

She took a deep breath.

"Suck it up, Demi," she said out loud to herself. "You knew what kind of guy he was when you met him. That's why you took him home." She couldn't be upset with him for being who he was. Or she could, but that would make her an asshole.

How's everything going? Everything going well with Gavin? No bad news or anything?

She hit Send, threw her phone on the bed, and tried to smother herself with her pillow for being such a wuss about texting someone.

Her phone rang, and she froze.

She fumbled for her cell and saw that it was Saxon.

Oh shit. She hadn't been prepared to actually speak to him.

"Play it cool, Demi. Play it cool."

Wuss.

"Hello?" she said as nonchalantly as possible.

"Hey."

She bit her lip. How had she missed how sexy his voice was?

"Hey," she said back.

"So, I thought Vance was keeping you up-to-date on everything. I thought he'd mentioned that he told you that Eldon was getting an award."

Crap. "Oh, he is. He did." *I just wanted to have an excuse to talk to you.* "I just hadn't heard from him for a few days, and I didn't want to bother him. I kind of have a thing I have to go to today, and I didn't want there to be any trouble."

"A thing?" It was a question, but he really didn't sound that interested.

She might as well tell him. Trying to get a guy to fish for answers wasn't who she was.

"Don't be jealous. It's only a family birthday party for my younger sister."

"Oh." Saxon sounded genuinely surprised. "I didn't know you saw your family."

Demi rolled onto her back. "It's not very often, but my youngest sister is eighteen, and my mother wants me there. While I will be bored the entire time, I don't want any danger coming to my family. So, I thought I'd check with you."

Saxon didn't say anything.

Demi sighed. "Anyway, I'm sorry I bothered you. I'll see you…" Would she see him again? If she showed up at Club Seduction? Could she handle it if she didn't? Either way, she needed to figure out what to do about her heat because she didn't want to sleep with anyone else yet. And she couldn't go back to being once-a-month heat buddies with Saxon. "I mean, I'll see you around. Gotta go."

"Demi—"

"Bye." She quickly hit End and dropped her phone on her chest. "I am such a wuss," she said to her empty bedroom.

☾

Demi hit the doorbell of her mom and stepfather's house and then stood back, straightened her clothes, and smoothed down her hair. Her mother didn't really care about looks that much, but she always wanted to look her best.

The door swung open, and her sister, Stacy, opened the door.

"Hey you. You don't have to knock, silly." Stacy opened the door wide to let Demi in.

"I don't mind." She was not close enough to her mom and stepfather to simply walk into their house, even when she had been invited for a birthday party.

"I can take the present."

Stacy was the oldest of her half-sisters at twenty, and she had always been nice to Demi. Sometimes, it made her sad that they weren't closer, but her mother didn't want her sisters or stepfather to know she was half-shifter. It was easier to keep a distance between the two rather than hide that part of herself.

Demi put the small box in Stacy's hands. "Thank you."

"Come on in. You're one of the last to arrive. Stephanie will be happy to see you, seeing as how Aunt Carol won't stop talking about her latest visit to the doctor."

"Eh, that sounds fun," Demi said sarcastically.

Their mother's older sister was a hypochondriac and mistakenly thought everyone loved to hear her hospital stories.

Demi followed Stacy into the kitchen. When Stephanie saw her, her eyes lit up. Stacy hurried off, probably so she wouldn't get roped into a conversation with Aunt Carol, too.

"Demi, you're here." Stephanie pulled her into a hug. "Thank you for rescuing me."

"Happy birthday."

They separated.

"Thank you."

"I gave your present to Stacy. She said she'd put it in the pile."

"Demi."

She turned to see her mother entering the kitchen. "Hi, Mom."

Her mom pulled her into a hug. "It's good to see you."

"Thanks. You, too." It was mostly true. Despite their distance, this woman was still her mother.

"So, how is everything, Demi? How's work?" Aunt Carol asked as she took a sip of wine.

"Do you want anything to drink?" Stephanie asked.

"Yes, please." She looked at her aunt. "Things are good. Summers are always busy at the library."

"Any men in your life?" The way she asked came out condescending and judgmental. As if Aunt Carol were happily married. She and her husband acted more like coworkers than husband and wife.

"Well, actually—"

"Demi," Stacy said from the other room. "You didn't tell me your boyfriend was coming."

Boyfriend? She quickly tried to figure out who would show up at her mom's house.

Stacy walked into the kitchen with Saxon behind her.

Demi started to gasp but quickly recovered when all eyes went to her.

Saxon came up to Demi, put his arm around her, and kissed her on the forehead. "Sorry I'm late."

"Uh—that's—uh—yeah—that's okay," Demi said, stumbling over her words. "I thought you couldn't make it."

Saxon smiled. "I moved some things around."

Demi's mother cleared her throat. "Demi, are you going to introduce us?"

"Oh, yeah." She looked up into Saxon's handsome face. She had no idea why he was here, but she had never been more grateful to see him. "This is Saxon. Saxon, this is my mom, Sharon, my aunt Carol, and my sisters, Stacy and Stephanie."

Saxon shook each of their hands. "Happy birthday," he said to her little sister.

Stephanie blushed. "Thank you."

FORTY-THREE

EVERYONE LOVED SAXON, and Demi was amazed at his behavior because he'd really brought out the charm with her family. She'd had no idea he had it in him.

After what felt like a game of Twenty Questions, Demi decided it was time to figure out why Saxon was really there. Despite Saxon's laid-back attitude, her immediate thought was that she was in danger again, and if someone was after her, she wanted to leave as soon as she could. She didn't want anyone hurting her family.

"Can you all excuse us? I need to speak to Saxon alone for a second."

Stacy wiggled her eyebrows. "You can use my bedroom."

Demi laughed awkwardly. "That's okay. Thank you though."

She grabbed Saxon's hand and led him outside.

"What are you doing here? You just told me this morning that everything was okay." Demi did a three-sixty, trying to spot anything out of place.

Saxon put his hands on her arms. "Damn it. I'm an ass. I didn't even think that you'd jump to that conclusion." He shook his head and smiled. "But, knowing you, I should have guessed that's where your mind would go right away."

She scrunched up her nose. "I'm confused. Does that mean we're safe?"

Saxon laughed. "You're fine. Everything is the same as the way it was this morning."

Demi's body sagged with relief as she put a hand to her chest. "Thank God." She straightened. "But then, what are you doing here? How did you know where my mom lived?"

"Reid."

Of course.

"And I'm here for you. That's what mates or boyfriends do after all."

Demi shook her head. "But you're not my boyfriend or my mate."

Saxon pushed the collar of her blouse out of the way. "That's not what my bite mark says."

"Saxon, we both know we did that to keep me safe. It's not real."

He lifted his brow. "And what if I want it to be real?"

Demi opened her mouth, but she couldn't seem to find her words.

Saxon stepped forward and pulled her into his arms. "And, as I recall, we marked each other after we found out you were safe again. There was no secondary incentive."

Demi was desperate to believe everything Saxon had said, but she was scared. What if Saxon remembered that she was less than? What if he wanted a full shifter? What if she wasn't enough for him?

She lifted her chin. "That was my mistake. I shouldn't have led you on."

"You're saying you don't want me?"

She opened her mouth again.

"And don't lie to me." He tapped his nose. "I can smell it."

"Fine," she said like a bratty teenager. She'd just have to scare him away. "Yes, I want you. I don't want anyone else. I think I'm probably even in love with you."

Saxon grinned and clapped his hands together. "Great."

"Great?" She stomped her foot on the ground. "You're a confirmed bachelor. You're afraid of commitment."

"I don't remember ever saying I was afraid of commitment. It kind of grossed me out sometimes when couples got sappy, but I'm not afraid." He picked up her hands. "I think you're confusing me with you."

"Me?"

"Yeah, you. You're afraid I'm going to leave you, aren't you?"

"There is a possibility you'll get sick of me."

"Oh, I'm sure I'll get sick of you."

Demi's jaw dropped in outrage. He wasn't supposed to admit that.

Saxon laughed. "But, even if I'm sick of you, I will still love you. And I will still want you in my life forever."

"How do you know?"

"Because I've never felt about anybody the way I feel about you. You're never getting rid of me, Demi."

"Promise?"

"I promise. I love you."

Demi pushed herself into his arms and buried her face in his shirt. "I love you, too."

Saxon wrapped his arms around her. "I can't wait to show you the bunkhouse."

"I've already seen it," she said into his chest.

"Not since we've been working hard to add on the extra bedrooms."

Demi looked up at Saxon in surprise. "Already?"

Saxon smiled. "That's what happens when you own a construction company. You call in a few favors to get everything approved by the city, and then you make your employees work round the clock."

"Wow. But how did you work in the dark?"

"Big-ass lights."

Demi laughed. "Does this mean, we'll have our own room?" She was almost afraid to ask, worried that he'd tell her he'd been joking. But he'd promised her, and she had to trust him. Or at least, learn to try.

"Do you want to live there? You still have your house. My apartment. We could get rid of them both and buy something closer."

"You're leaving it up to me?"

"Yes. I want you to be happy. Wherever you go, I go."

She'd had no idea Saxon could be so sweet. She had to fight back tears. She swallowed down her crying. She could do that later. "I think I'd like to live at the bunkhouse. I liked living with others who are like me."

"Bunkhouse it is then."

Demi reached her mouth up and kissed him. She pulled back and decided to give him one more test. "If we choose bunkhouse, it doesn't have to be that way forever, right?"

"Right. We might get sick of everyone in a few years."

"Or we might have a kid or two and want our own place."

Saxon didn't even flinch. "Maybe." He winced. "But let's keep that information quiet right now. If my mother even gets a whiff of grandchildren, she will hound me every day."

"Your mother, huh?"

"Oh, yeah. She's going to fucking love you."

"I can't wait to meet her."

☽

Saxon brought Demi into the bunkhouse and paused to listen for any sounds. He had warned some of them that he was bringing her home and to not make a big deal out of it, but he wouldn't put it past his friends to jump out and yell, *Surprise*.

"What's wrong?" she asked him.

"Nothing. I was just wondering who else was here. Come on."

"Did you get a new room, or do you have your old one?"

"*We* got a new room. Camden gets the old one."

"Exciting. I love new-paint smell."

Saxon showed her down the new hallway. The bunkhouse before had been shaped like a capital T. Instead of making the hall longer, they had put another hall on the opposite side of the kitchen and living room, making the bunkhouse shaped like a plus sign or cross now.

"Here it is," Saxon said, pushing the door open.

"Wow. It's so big."

"It's the same size as the other rooms. It just looks huge now that there is only one bed. This way, we have plenty of room to set up our own little living area." He walked over to the corner. "I thought we could maybe put a chair here or something and our own TV, so we can be alone when we want to."

Demi stared at him, and he could not read her expression.

"What is it?"

"You've really thought about this."

He shrugged. "Why wouldn't I? I want it to be perfect for you."

Demi ran to him and jumped into his arms.

"Oof."

She smiled down at him. "I love you."

"I love you, too." He licked his lips and gave her a heated look. "What do you say we christen the place?"

"You're on."

☾

Down the hall and across the living room, Kendall lay on her bed with her tablet on her lap. She typed her keywords into the search engine until she found what she had been searching for.

Local Detective Earns Award

She clicked on the video to make it play. It was a video of Eldon being honored by the chief of police for his work in his brother's arrest. His abduction had probably had something to do with it.

Kendall rubbed her little bump. "That's your daddy right there, little one. I wonder what he's going to do when I tell him about you."

That was a conversation she was not looking forward to.

EPILOGUE

SEVERAL MONTHS LATER

"COME ON, baby. I know you can do it," Saxon chanted to urge Demi on. He was her biggest cheerleader and believed in her more than she believed in herself sometimes.

She took a deep breath, closed her eyes, and concentrated. She reached deep down inside—although not as deep as she'd once had to—and connected with her cat.

Let's do this, her cat said, and a feeling like she'd been hit by lightning went through her body.

Saxon whooped loudly, and she opened her eyes.

She took a step back because everything looked weird, and she fell on her butt.

Saxon laughed.

I'm not used to having four legs, she said. Or tried to. It came out as a weird half-meow, half-growl.

Saxon laughed again. "You'll get used to not being able to talk." He walked over to her and crouched down on his knees. "You are a beautiful golden color," he said as he rubbed her ears.

Damn. That felt really good.

She looked down at her legs. She could still see colors, but they were muted and not as bright. She'd have to take Saxon's word for it.

"I knew you could shift."

And he was right. It had taken a lot of work, but here she was, and it was amazing.

Saxon petted her from head to butt and wondered if it was a weird thing to have your mate pet you. She needed to ask one of the girls because it made her feel a little like a kid.

Demi pushed her head into Saxon's chest.

"You want me to shift with you?"

She nodded.

"Deal."

☾

After running for what had to be a good hour, Demi and Saxon collapsed on the grass where they'd left their clothes. They often went running and took naps outside when they were done. But they hadn't been able to do that as much now that the weather was getting cold.

Saxon shifted back, and it suddenly occurred to Demi that she could get stuck in her cat form.

Saxon put his hand on her head. "Just think about your human form again. You can do it."

Demi closed her eyes again, and almost immediately, the same feeling of lightning struck. She opened her eyes and laughed. "That was easier than I'd thought it would be." Demi kissed him. "Thank you for helping me."

Saxon grinned at her. "No thanks needed. I always knew you could do it."

The two stood and got dressed.

"I can't wait for next spring. We're coming out here every day," she told him.

"I'm going to hold you to it."

Saxon put his arm around her and walked her back to the bunkhouse. "What do you have going on the rest of today?"

"I have to meet Siya for dinner, but that's it."

"That's right. Do you think she'll ever come around here again?"

Demi shrugged. "Who knows? She just tells me she's not comfortable with doing it."

It made it harder sometimes to keep up their friendship, but it was worth it. Siya had always been there for her, and Demi loved her like a sister. Probably more than she loved her own.

"When you come home, let's stay in and cuddle," Saxon said and nuzzled her ear.

Demi smiled. When she'd met him in Club Seduction, she'd never taken him for a snuggler, but it turned out that he loved it.

"You've got yourself a date," she said.

They reached the bunkhouse, and Saxon looked down at her. "I'm so glad I seduced you all those months ago, Demi Cross Einar."

Demi laughed. "Ha. That's what you think, but you have it wrong. I'm the one who seduced you."

FORBIDDEN MATE SAMPLE

Quentin Rawling exited the gate at the Minneapolis-St. Paul International Airport and headed down to baggage claim. He hadn't realized how much he had missed Minneapolis until his plane landed. While he had been glad that he could help his sister and parents by going with her to the rehab facility in Switzerland, he was happy to be home.

For the last month of his sister's yearlong treatment, she was in the center, alone. Patients did this to learn to rely on themselves and to trust that they could make good decisions on their own. Or something like that. But it only happened if the patients were doing well in treatment, which his sister was.

So, while Larissa had one month left before she would come back, Quentin was home a month earlier than he'd originally thought when he left the country.

His phone buzzed in his pocket.

Jeremiah: I'm here, waiting for you.

Quentin grinned down at his phone.

While Switzerland was beautiful and had many English

speakers, he'd felt lonely and like an outsider. He saw his sister every day, but she was regularly tied up with her treatment, so he often had hours to himself.

It took him less than a week to find a local coffee shop and become a regular. While the workers and other customers became acquaintances of his and people he could bullshit with, none of them were true friends. And Quentin started feeling homesick.

About two months in, he was sitting in his usual spot when he heard an American accent. Not only was the guy an American, but he was also from Minnesota and a wolf-shifter. Just like Quentin.

Normally, he probably wouldn't have been so bold, but the second the guy was handed his order, Quentin approached him.

And that was how he'd met Jeremiah.

Jeremiah had gotten to the treatment facility with his mother—supporting her the same way Quentin supported his sister—a month and a half before Quentin. It was kind of crazy that it had taken them two months to run into each other.

Unfortunately, because Jeremiah had arrived a month and a half prior to Quentin, this meant he had gone back home a month and a half earlier, too, as his mom had also done well in treatment. The last few weeks had been hard on Quentin, even with his sister having more and more free time.

Quentin: I'll be out as soon as I grab my luggage.

"Hey."

Quentin looked up to see Jeremiah standing five feet away. His dark hair was cut shorter than the last time

Quentin had seen him, but his green eyes exuded the same warmth he remembered.

Quentin broke out in a grin as he hurried to Jeremiah and hugged him. "I thought you were going to wait in the car."

Jeremiah smiled and shook his head. "I wanted to see you as soon as possible."

"I missed you," Quentin said with a sigh.

"I missed you, too."

Quentin grabbed the front of Jeremiah's shirt and yanked him close, so he could kiss him. He smiled against the other man's mouth. "Thanks for coming to pick me up."

He let go of Jeremiah's shirt and headed for the baggage carousel.

"You know I wouldn't have missed it. I needed a break from my mother."

"How's she doing?"

Jeremiah's mom had been home for two weeks. She had been alone at the center the last month, too, but her treatment was done now, and Quentin imagined it must have been an adjustment for her, being back in the States.

"Good. I made sure to clean out her house before she got back to Minnesota. No liquor anywhere. The only problem now is, she doesn't have anything to do. Drinking was her only hobby." Jeremiah rolled his eyes. "And now, it's hanging out with her son. I would have come to the airport no matter what, so I could get some time away."

Quentin laughed. "You'll have to help her find some new friends and things to do. I'm sure there's a senior center not too far from her house somewhere."

Jeremiah scratched his chin. "She said absolutely no bingo."

"Senior centers do more than just bingo. Some can even help people find places to volunteer."

Jeremiah dropped his hand. "Thanks. How do you know all this anyway?"

"It's part of the job."

"Which one?"

Quentin thought about it for a second. "Both."

Even with finding Jeremiah in Europe, he had still felt like a piece of himself was missing while he was there. His work. He loved being a sentinel, and he loved being a police officer. He couldn't wait to get back to both his jobs.

"Is that your suitcase?" Jeremiah asked, pointing to a large black one coming down the chute.

"How'd you know?" Quentin joked.

"It's the only suitcase big enough to hold months' worth of clothes."

Quentin pulled his luggage off the carousel with ease. "Yet it felt like I was doing laundry every other day."

"Same."

Quentin smiled. "Lead the way to your car."

"This way," Jeremiah said, pointing to one of the double doors.

Quentin noticed that Jeremiah's mood had suddenly changed. "You okay?"

Jeremiah took a deep breath. "Yeah. Super nervous about meeting the alpha."

That would explain it.

"I told you, Damien is cool. He's young and progressive. You don't have to be worried."

"Easier said than done."

"You'll see when we get there."

"Is there anyone I need to be worried about?"

An image of Hunter flashed through Quentin's brain, but he immediately pushed the vampire from his mind. Hunter didn't want to be with him, so he shouldn't have a problem with Quentin bringing someone home.

"Nope," Quentin told Jeremiah. "Everyone's super cool, and they already know I'm gay. They're going to love you."

Order Now!

ABOUT THE AUTHOR

R.L. Kenderson is two best friends writing under one name.

Renae has always loved reading, and in third grade, she wrote her first poem where she learned she might have a knack for this writing thing. Lara remembers sneaking her grandmother's Harlequin novels when she was probably too young to be reading them, and since then, she knew she wanted to write her own.

When they met in college, they bonded over their love of reading and the TV show *Charmed*. What really spiced up their friendship was when Lara introduced Renae to romance novels. When they discovered their first vampire romance, they knew there would always be a special place in their hearts for paranormal romance. After being unable to find certain storylines and characteristics they wanted to read about in the hundreds of books they consumed, they decided to write their own.

One lives in the Minneapolis-St. Paul area and the other in the Kansas City area where they're a sonographer/stay-at-home mom/wife and pharmacist/mother by day, and together they're a sexy author by night. They communicate through phone, email, and whole lot of messaging.

You can find them at http://www.rlkenderson.com, Facebook, Instagram, TikTok, Twitter, and Goodreads. Join their reader group! Or you can email them at rlkenderson@ rlkenderson.com, or sign up for their newsletter. They always love hearing from their readers.